ME

THE ORIENTAL STORY BOOK - A COLLECTION OF TALES

THE BEST BOOKS OF FAIRY TALES

by Wilhelm Hauff

THE ORIENTAL STORY BOOK: A COLLECTION OF TALES

Contributions by Merlin Books

First Printing: 1855

As you know, the new is a well-forgotten old. This also applies to books. And how much joy there is when parents (and also grandparents!) find out in the newly printed books the editions of their childhood - with the same illustrations! This is how the generations are connected: the elders remember their childhood - and share their memories with the younger ones ...

Wilhelm Hauff was a German poet and novelist. Considering his brief life, Hauff was an extraordinarily prolific writer. The freshness and originality of his talent, his inventiveness, and his genial humour have won him a high place among the southern German prose writers of the early nineteenth century.

Cover designed by Freepik

TOC

THE CARAVAN

INTRODUCTION

IN a beautiful distant kingdom, of which there is a saying, that the sun on its everlasting green gardens never goes down, ruled, from the beginning of time even to the present day, Queen Phantasie. With full hands, she used to distribute for many hundred years, the abundance of her blessings among her subjects, and was beloved and respected by all who knew her. The heart of the Queen, however, was too great to allow her to stop at her own land with her charities; she herself, in the royal attire of her everlasting youth and beauty, descended upon the earth; for she had heard that there men lived, who passed their lives in sorrowful seriousness, in the midst of care and toil. Unto these she had sent the finest gifts out of her kingdom, and ever since the beauteous Queen came through the fields of earth, men were merry at their labor, and happy in their seriousness.

Her children, moreover, not less fair and lovely than their royal mother, she had sent forth to bring happiness to men. One day Märchen[1], the eldest daughter of the Queen, came back in haste from the earth. The mother observed that Märchen was sorrowful; yes, at times it would seem to her as if her eyes would be consumed by weeping.

"What is the matter with thee, beloved Märchen?" said the Queen to her. "Ever since thy journey, thou art so sorrowful and dejected; wilt thou not confide to thy mother what ails thee?"

---

[1] Märchen represents the fairy or legendary tales, of which the Germans were at one time so fond.

"Ah! dear mother," answered Märchen, "I would have kept silence, had I not known that my sorrow is thine also."

"Speak, my daughter!" entreated the fair Queen. "Grief is a stone, which presses down him who bears it alone, but two draw it lightly out of the way."

"Thou wishest it," rejoined Märchen, "so listen. Thou knowest how gladly I associate with men, how cheerfully I sit down before the huts of the poor, to while away a little hour for them after their labor; formerly, when I came, they used to ask me kindly for my hand to salute, and looked upon me afterwards, when I went away, smiling and contented; but in these days, it is so no longer!"

"Poor Märchen!" said the Queen as she caressed her cheek, which was wet with a tear. "But, perhaps, thou only fanciest all this."

"Believe me, I feel it but too well," rejoined Märchen; "they love me no more. Wherever I go, cold looks meet me; nowhere am I any more gladly seen; even the children, who ever loved me so well, laugh at me, and slyly turn their backs upon me."

The Queen leaned her forehead on her hand, and was silent in reflection. "And how, then, Märchen," she asked, "should it happen that the people there below have become so changed?"

"See, O Queen Phantasie! men have stationed vigilant watchmen, who inspect and examine all that comes from thy kingdom, with sharp eyes. If one should arrive who is not according to their mind, they raise a loud cry, and put him to death, or else so slander him to men, who believe their every word, that one finds no longer any love, any little ray of confidence. Ah! how fortunate are my brothers, the Dreams! they leap merrily and lightly down upon the earth, care nothing for those artful men, seek the slumbering, and weave and paint for them, what makes happy the heart, and brightens the eye with joy."

"Thy brothers are light-footed," said the Queen, "and thou, my darling, hast no reason for envying them. Besides, I know these border-watchmen well; men are not so wrong in sending them out; there came so many boastful fellows, who acted as if they had come straight from my kingdom, and yet they had, at best, only looked down upon us from some mountain."

"But why did they make me, thine own daughter, suffer for this?" wept forth Märchen. "Ah, if thou knewest how they have acted towards me! They called me an old maid, and threatened the next time not to admit me!"

"How, my daughter?—not to admit thee more?" asked the Queen, as anger heightened the color on her cheeks. "But already I see whence this comes; that wicked cousin has slandered us!"

"Fashion? Impossible!" exclaimed Märchen; "she always used to act so friendly towards us."

"Oh, I know her, the false one!" answered the Queen. "But try it again in spite of her, my daughter: whoever wishes to do good, must not rest."

"Ah, mother! suppose, then, they send me back again, or slander me so that men let me stay in a corner, disregarded, or alone and slighted!"

"If the old, deluded by Fashion, value thee at nothing, then turn thee to the young; truly they are my little favorites. I send to them my loveliest pictures through thy brothers, the Dreams; yes, already I have often hovered over them in person, caressed and kissed them, and played fine games with them. They, also, know me well, though not by name; for I have often observed how in the night they laugh at my stars, and in the morning, when my shining fleeces play over the heavens, how they clap their hands for joy. Moreover, when they grow larger, they love me still; then I help the charming maids to weave variegated garlands, and the wild boys to become still, while I seat myself near them, on the lofty summit of a cliff, steep lofty cities and brilliant palaces in the mist-world of the blue mountains in the distance, and, on the red-tinged clouds of evening, paint brave troops of horsemen, and strange pilgrim processions."

"Oh, the dear children!" exclaimed Märchen, deeply affected. "Yes—be it so! with them I will make one more trial."

"Yes, my good child," answered the Queen; "go unto them; but I will attire thee in fine style, that thou mayest please the little ones, and that the old may not drive thee away. See! the dress of an Almanach[2] will I give thee."

"An Almanach, mother? Ah!—I will be ashamed to parade, in such a way, before the people."

The Queen gave the signal, and the attendants brought in the rich dress of an Almanach. It was inwrought with brilliant colors, and beautiful figures. The waiting-maids plaited the long hair of the fair girl, bound golden sandals on her feet, and arrayed her in the robe.

The modest Märchen dared not look up; her mother, however, beheld her with satisfaction, and clasped her in her arms. "Go forth!" said she unto the little one; "my blessing be with thee. If they despise and scorn thee, turn quickly unto me; perhaps later generations, more true to nature, may again incline to thee their hearts."

Thus spoke Queen Phantasie, while Märchen went down upon the earth. With beating heart she approached the city, in which the cunning watchmen dwelt: she dropped her head towards the earth, wrapped her fine robe closely around her, and with trembling step drew near unto the gate.

"Hold!" exclaimed a deep, rough voice. "Look out, there! Here comes a new Almanach!"

Märchen trembled as she heard this; many old men, with gloomy countenances, rushed forth; they had sharp quills in their fists,

---

[2] The German "Almanach" corresponds in a measure with the English "Annual."

and held them towards Märchen. One of the multitude strode up to her, and seized her with rough hand by the chin. "Just lift up your head, Mr. Almanach," he cried, "that one may see in your eyes whether you be right or not."

Blushing, Märchen lifted her little head quite up, and raised her dark eye.

"Märchen!" exclaimed the watchmen, laughing boisterously. "Märchen! That we should have had any doubt as to who was here! How come you, now, by this dress?"

"Mother put it on me," answered Märchen.

"So! she wishes to smuggle you past us! Not this time! Out of the way; see that you be gone!" exclaimed the watchmen among themselves, lifting up their sharp quills.

"But, indeed, I will go only to the children," entreated Märchen; "this, surely, you will grant to me."

"Stay there not, already, enough of these menials in the land around?" exclaimed one of the watchmen. "They only prattle nonsense to our children."

"Let us see what she knows this time," said another.

"Well then," cried they, "tell us what you know; but make haste, for we have not much time for you."

Märchen stretched forth her hand, and described with the forefinger, various figures in the air. Thereupon they saw confused images move slowly across it;—caravans, fine horses, riders gayly attired, numerous tents upon the sand of the desert; birds, and ships upon the stormy seas; silent forests, and populous places, and highways; battles, and peaceful wandering tribes—all hovered, a motley crowd, in animated pictures, over before them.

Märchen, in the eagerness with which she had caused the figures to rise forth, had not observed that the watchmen of the gate had one by one fallen asleep. Just as she was about to describe new lines, a friendly man came up to her, and seized her hand. "Look here, good Märchen," said he, as he pointed to the sleepers; "for these thy varied creations are as nothing; slip nimbly through the door; they will not suspect that thou art in the land, and thou canst quietly and unobserved pursue thy way. I will lead thee unto my children; in my house will give thee a peaceful, friendly home; there thou mayest remain and live by thyself; whenever my sons and daughters shall have learned their lessons well, they shall be permitted to run to thee with their plays, and attend to thee. Dost thou agree?"

"Oh! how gladly will I follow thee unto thy dear children! how diligently will I endeavor to make, at times, for them, a happy little hour!"

The good man nodded to her cordially, and assisted her to step over the feet of the sleeping men. Märchen, when she had got safely across, looked around smilingly, and then slipped quickly through the gate.

THE CARAVAN

ONCE upon a time, there marched through the wilderness a large Caravan. Upon the vast plain, where one sees nothing but sand and heaven, were heard already, in the far distance, the little bells of the camels, and the silver-toned ones of the horses; a thick cloud of dust, which preceded them, announced their approach, and when a gale of wind separated the clouds, glittering weapons and brilliant dresses dazzled the eye. Such was the appearance of the Caravan to a man who was riding up towards it in an oblique direction. He was mounted on a fine Arabian courser, covered with a tiger-skin; silver bells were suspended from the deep-red stripe work, and on the head of the horse waved a plume of heron feathers. The rider was of majestic mien, and his attire corresponded with the splendor of his horse: a white turban, richly inwrought with gold, adorned his head, his habit and wide pantaloons were of bright red, and a curved sword with a magnificent handle hung by his side. He had arranged the turban far down upon his forehead; this, together with the dark eyes which gleamed forth from under his bushy brows, and the long beard which hung down under his arched nose, gave him a wild, daring expression. When the horseman had advanced fifty paces farther, the foremost line of the Caravan was near, and putting spurs to his steed, in the twinkling of an eye he was at the head of the procession. It was so unusual a thing to see a solitary rider travelling through the desert, that the guard, apprehending an attack, put their lances in rest.

"What mean you?" exclaimed the horseman, as he saw himself received in so hostile a manner. "Do you imagine that a single man would attack your Caravan?"

Ashamed of their precipitation, the guards lowered their lances, and their leader rode forth to the stranger, and asked to know his pleasure.

"Who is the lord of this Caravan?" inquired the cavalier.

"It belongs to no single lord," answered the interrogated one; "but to several merchants, who march from Mecca to their native country, and whom we escort through the desert; for oftentimes scoundrels of every kind alarm those who travel here."

"Then lead me to the merchants," responded the stranger.

"That cannot be now," rejoined the other, "for we must proceed without delay, and the merchants are at least a quarter of a mile behind; if, however, you would like to ride along with me until we halt to take our siesta, I will execute your desire."

The stranger said nothing further; he drew forth a long pipe which he had attached to his saddle, and began to smoke with slow puffs, as he rode along by the leader of the van. The latter knew not what to make of the stranger, and ventured not to ask his name in so many words; but when he artfully endeavored to weave up a conversation, the cavalier, to his remarks, "You smoke there a good tobacco," or, "Your horse has a brave gait," constantly replied with only a brief "Yes, yes!" At last they arrived at the place where they were to halt for the siesta: the chief sent his people forward to keep a look-out, while he remained with the stranger to receive the Caravan. First, thirty camels passed by, heavily laden, guided by armed drivers. After these, on fine horses, came the five merchants to whom the Caravan belonged. They were, for the most part, men of advanced age, of grave and serious aspect; one, however, seemed much younger, as well as more gay and lively than the rest. A large number of camels and pack-horses closed the procession.

Tents were pitched, and the camels and horses fastened around. In the midst was a large pavilion of blue silk, to which the chief of the escort conducted the stranger. When they reached the entrance, they saw the five merchants seated on gold-embroidered cushions; black slaves were carrying around to them food and drink. "Whom bringest thou hither to us?" exclaimed the young merchant unto the leader: before, however, the latter could reply, the stranger spoke.

"I am called Selim Baruch, and am from Bagdad; I was taken captive by a robber-horde on a ride to Mecca, but three days ago managed to free myself from confinement. The mighty Prophet permitted me to hear, in the far distance, the little bells of your Caravan, and so I came to you. Allow me to ride in your company; you will grant your protection to no unworthy person; and when we reach Bagdad, I will reward your kindness richly, for I am the nephew of the Grand Vizier."

The oldest of the merchants took up the discourse: "Selim Baruch," said he, "welcome to our protection! It affords us joy to be of assistance to thee. But first of all, sit down, and eat and drink with us."

Selim Baruch seated himself among the merchants, and ate and drank with them. After the meal, the slaves removed the table, and brought long pipes and Turkish sherbet. The merchants sat for some time in silence, while they puffed out before them the bluish, smoke-clouds, watching how they formed circle after circle, and at last were dissipated in the ambient air. The young merchant finally broke the silence. "Here sit we for three days," said he, "on horseback, and at table, without doing any thing to while away the time. I feel this tediousness much, for I am accustomed after dinner to see dancers, or to hear singing and music. Know you nothing, my friends, that will pass away the time for us?"

The four elder merchants smoked away, and seemed to be seriously reflecting, but the stranger spoke: "If it be allowed me, I will make a proposition to you. I think one of us, at this resting-place, could relate something for the amusement of the rest: this, certainly, would serve to pass the time."

"Selim Baruch, thou hast well spoken," said Achmet, the oldest of the merchants; "let us accept the proposal."

"I am rejoiced that it pleases you," answered Selim; "and, in order that you may see that I desire nothing unreasonable, I will myself begin." The five merchants, overjoyed, drew nearer together, and placed the stranger in their midst. The slaves replenished their cups, filled the pipes of their masters afresh, and brought glowing coals for a light. Selim cleared his voice with a hearty draught of sherbet, smoothed back the long beard from his mouth, and said, "Listen then to the History of Caliph Stork."

THE HISTORY OF CALIPH STORK

CHAPTER I

ONCE upon a time, on a fine afternoon, the Caliph Chasid was seated on his sofa in Bagdad: he had slept a little, (for it was a hot day,) and now, after his nap, looked quite happy. He smoked a long pipe of rosewood, sipped, now and then, a little coffee which a slave poured out for him, and stroked his beard, well-satisfied, for the flavor pleased him. In a word, it was evident that the Caliph was in a good humor. At this season one could easily speak with him, for he was always very mild and affable; on which account did his Grand-Vizier, Mansor, seek him at this hour, every day.

On the afternoon in question he also came, but looked very serious, quite contrary to his usual custom. The Caliph removed the pipe, a moment, from his mouth, and said, "Wherefore, Grand-Vizier, wearest thou so thoughtful a visage?"

The Grand-Vizier folded his arms crosswise over his breast,

made reverence to his lord, and answered: "Sir, whether I wear a thoughtful look, I know not, but there, below the palace, stands a trader who has such fine goods, that it vexes me not to have abundant money."

The Caliph, who had often before this gladly indulged his Vizier, sent down his black slave to bring up the merchant, and in a moment they entered together. He was a short, fat man, of swarthy countenance and tattered dress. He carried a chest in which were all kinds of wares—pearls and rings, richly-wrought pistols, goblets, and combs. The Caliph and his Vizier examined them all, and the former at length purchased fine pistols for himself and Mansor, and a comb for the Vizier's wife. When the pedler was about to close his chest, the Caliph espied a little drawer, and inquired whether there were wares in that also. The trader drew forth the drawer, and pointed out therein a box of black powder, and a paper with strange characters, which neither the Caliph nor Mansor could read.

"I obtained these two articles, some time ago, from a merchant, who found them in the street at Mecca," said the trader. "I know not what they contain. They are at your service for a moderate price; I can do nothing with them." The Caliph, who gladly kept old manuscripts in his library, though he could not read them, purchased writing and box, and discharged the merchant. The Caliph, however, thought he would like to know what the writing contained, and asked the Vizier if he knew any one who could decipher it.

"Most worthy lord and master," answered he, "near the great Mosque lives a man called 'Selim the Learned,' who understands all languages: let him come, perhaps he is acquainted with these mysterious characters."

The learned Selim was soon brought in. "Selim," said the Caliph to him, "Selim, they say thou art very wise; look a moment at this manuscript, and see if thou canst read it. If thou canst, thou shalt receive from me a new festival-garment; if not, thou shalt have twelve blows on the cheek, and five and twenty on the soles of the feet, since, in that case, thou art unjustly called Selim the Learned."

Selim bowed himself and said, "Sire, thy will be done!" For a long time he pored over the manuscript, but suddenly exclaimed, "This is Latin, sire, or I will suffer myself to be hung."

"If it is Latin, tell us what is therein," commanded the Caliph. Selim began to translate:—

"Man, whosoever thou mayest be that findest this, praise Allah for his goodness! Whoever snuffs of the dust of this powder, and at the same time says, Mutabor, can change himself into any animal, and shall also understand its language. If he wishes to return to the form of a man, then let him bow three times to the East, and repeat the same word. But take thou care, if thou be transformed, that thou laugh not; otherwise shall the magic word fade altogether from thy remembrance, and thou shalt remain a beast!"

When Selim the Learned had thus read, the Caliph was overjoyed. He made the translator swear to tell no one of their secret, presented him a beautiful garment, and discharged him. To his Grand-Vizier, however, he said: "That I call a good purchase, Mansor! How can I contain myself until I become an animal! Early in the morning, do thou come to me. Then will we go together into the country, take a little snuff out of my box, and hear what is said in the air and in the water, in the forest and in the field."

CHAPTER II

SCARCELY, on the next morning, had the Caliph Chasid breakfasted and dressed himself, when the Grand-Vizier appeared, to accompany him, as he had commanded, on his walk. The Caliph placed the box with the magic powder in his girdle, and having commanded his train to remain behind, set out, all alone with Mansor, upon their expedition. They went at first through the extensive gardens of the Caliph, but looked around in vain for some living thing, in order to make their strange experiment. The Vizier finally proposed to go farther on, to a pond, where he had often before seen many storks, which, by their grave behavior and clattering, had always excited his attention. The Caliph approved of the proposition of his

Vizier, and went with him to the pond. When they reached it they saw a stork walking gravely to and fro, seeking for frogs, and now and then clattering at something before her. Presently they saw, too, another stork hovering far up in the air.

"I will wager my beard, most worthy sire," exclaimed the Grand-Vizier, "that these two long-feet are even now carrying on a fine conversation with one another. How would it be, if we should become storks?"

"Well spoken!" answered the Caliph. "But first, we will consider how we may become men again.—Right! Three times bow to the East, and exclaim 'Mutabor!' then will I be Caliph once more, and thou Vizier. Only, for the sake of Heaven, laugh not, or we are lost!"

While the Caliph was thus speaking, he saw the other stork hovering over their heads, and sinking slowly to the ground. He drew the box quickly out of his girdle, and took a good pinch; then he presented it to the Grand-Vizier, who also snuffed some of the powder, and both exclaimed "Mutabor!" Immediately their legs shrivelled away and became slender and red; the handsome yellow slippers of the Caliph and his companion became misshapen stork's feet; their arms turned to wings; the neck extended up from the shoulders, and was an ell long; their beards had vanished, and their whole bodies were covered with soft feathers.

"You have a beautiful beak, my lord Grand-Vizier," exclaimed the Caliph after long astonishment. "By the beard of the Prophet, in my whole life I have not seen any thing like it!"

"Most humble thanks!" responded the Vizier, as he bowed. "But if I dared venture it, I might assert that your Highness looks almost as handsome when a stork, as when a Caliph. But suppose, if it be pleasing to you, that we observe and listen to our comrades, to see, if we actually understand Storkish."

Meanwhile the other stork reached the earth. He cleaned his feet with his bill, smoothed his feathers, and moved towards the first.

Both the new birds, thereupon, made haste to draw near, and to their astonishment, heard the following conversation.

"Good-morning, Madam Long-legs; already, so early, upon the pond?"

"Fine thanks, beloved Clatter-beak. I have brought me a little breakfast. Would you like, perhaps, the quarter of an eider-duck, or a little frog's thigh?"

"My best thanks, but this morning I have little appetite. I come to the pond for a very different reason. I have to dance to-day before the guests of my father, and I wish to practise a little in private."

Immediately, thereupon, the young lady-stork stepped, in great excitement, over the plain. The Caliph and Mansor looked on her in amazement. When, however, she stood in a picturesque attitude upon one foot, and, at the same time, gracefully moved her wings like a fan, the two could contain themselves no longer; a loud laugh broke forth from their bills. The Caliph was the first to recover himself. "That were once a joke," said he, "which gold could not have purchased. Pity! that the stupid birds should have been driven away by our laughter; otherwise they would certainly even yet have been singing."

But already it occurred to the Grand-Vizier that, during their metamorphosis, laughter was prohibited; he shared his anxiety on this head with the Caliph. "By Mecca and Medina! that were a sorry jest, if I am to remain a stork. Bethink thyself, then, of the foolish word, for I can recall it not."

"Three times must we bow ourselves to the East, and at the same time say, Mu—mu—mu—"

They turned to the East, and bowed so low that their beaks almost touched the earth. But, O misery! that magic word had escaped them; and though the Caliph prostrated himself again and again, though at the same time the Vizier earnestly cried "Mu—mu—," all recollection thereof had vanished, and poor Chasid and his Vizier were to remain storks.

CHAPTER III

THE enchanted ones wandered sorrowfully through the fields, not knowing, in their calamity, what they should first set about. To the city they could not return, for the purpose of discovering themselves, for who would have believed a stork that he was the Caliph? or, if he should find credit, would the inhabitants of Bagdad have been willing to have such a bird for their master? Thus, for several days, did they wander around, supporting themselves on the produce of the fields, which, however, on account of their long bills, they could not readily pick up. For eider-ducks and frogs they had no appetite, for they feared with such dainty morsels to ruin their stomachs. In this pitiable situation their only consolation was that they could fly, and accordingly they often winged their way to the roofs of Bagdad, to see what was going on therein.

On the first day they observed great commotion and mourning in the streets; but on the fourth after their transformation, they lighted by chance upon the royal palace, from which they saw, in the street beneath, a splendid procession. Drums and fifes sounded; on a richly-caparisoned steed was seated a man, in a scarlet mantle embroidered with gold, surrounded by gorgeously-attired attendants. Half Bagdad was running after him, crying, "Hail, Mizra! Lord of Bagdad!" All this the two storks beheld from the roof of the palace, and the Caliph Chasid exclaimed,—

"Perceivest thou now why I am enchanted, Grand-Vizier? This Mizra is the son of my deadly enemy, the mighty sorcerer Kaschnur, who, in an evil hour, vowed revenge against me. Still I do not abandon all hope. Come with me, thou faithful companion of my misery; we will go to the grave of the Prophet; perhaps in that holy spot the charm may be dissolved." They raised themselves from the roof of the palace, and flew in the direction of Medina.

In the use of their wings, however, they experienced some difficulty, for the two storks had, as yet, but little practice. "O Sire!"

groaned out the Vizier, after a couple of hours; "with your permission, I can hold out no longer; you fly so rapidly! Besides, it is already evening, and we would do well to seek a shelter for the night."

Chasid gave ear to the request of his attendant, and thereupon saw, in the vale beneath, a ruin which appeared to promise safe lodgings; and thither, accordingly, they flew. The place where they had alighted for the night, seemed formerly to have been a castle. Gorgeous columns projected from under the rubbish, and several chambers, which were still in a state of tolerable preservation, testified to the former magnificence of the mansion. Chasid and his companion went around through the corridor, to seek for themselves a dry resting-place; suddenly the stork Mansor paused. "Lord and master," he whispered softly, "were it not foolish for a Grand-Vizier, still more for a stork, to be alarmed at spectres, my mind is very uncomfortable; for here, close at hand, sighs and groans are very plainly perceptible." The Caliph now in turn stood still, and quite distinctly heard a low moaning, which seemed to belong rather to a human being than a beast. Full of expectation, he essayed to proceed to the place whence the plaintive sounds issued: but the Vizier, seizing him by the wing with his beak, entreated him fervently not to plunge them in new and unknown dangers. In vain! the Caliph, to whom a valiant heart beat beneath his stork-wing, burst away with the loss of a feather, and hastened into a gloomy gallery. In a moment he reached a door, which seemed only on the latch, and out of which he heard distinct sighs, accompanied by a low moaning. He pushed the door open with his bill, but stood, chained by amazement, upon the threshold. In the ruinous apartment, which was now but dimly lighted through a grated window, he saw a huge screech-owl sitting on the floor. Big tears rolled down from her large round eyes, and with ardent voice she sent her cries forth from her crooked bill. As soon, however, as she espied the Caliph and his Vizier, who meanwhile had crept softly up behind, she raised a loud cry of joy. She neatly wiped away the tears with her brown-striped wing, and to the great astonishment of both, exclaimed, in good human Arabic,—

"Welcome to you, storks! you are to me a good omen of deliverance, for it was once prophesied to me that, through storks, a great piece of good fortune is to fall to my lot."

When the Caliph recovered from his amazement, he bowed his long neck, brought his slender feet into an elegant position, and said: "Screech-owl, after your words, I venture to believe that I see in you a companion in misfortune. But, alas! this hope that through us thy deliverance will take place, is groundless. Thou wilt, thyself, realize our helplessness, when thou hearest our history."

The Screech-owl entreated him to impart it to her, and the Caliph, raising himself up, related what we already know.

CHAPTER IV

WHEN the Caliph had told his history to the owl, she thanked him, and said: "Listen to my story, also, and hear how I am no less unfortunate than thyself. My father is the king of India; I, his only, unfortunate daughter, am called Lusa. That same sorcerer Kaschnur, who transformed you, has plunged me also in this affliction. He came, one day, to my father, and asked me in marriage for his son Mizra. My father, however, who is a passionate man, cast him down the steps. The wretch managed to creep up to me again under another form, and as I was on one occasion taking the fresh air in my garden, clad as a slave, he presented me a potion which changed me into this detestable figure. He brought me hither, swooning through fear, and exclaimed in my ear with awful voice, 'There shalt thou remain, frightful one, despised even by beasts, until thy death, or till one, of his own free will, even under this execrable form, take thee to wife. Thus revenge I myself upon thee, and thy haughty father!'

"Since then, many months have elapsed; alone and mournfully I live, like a hermit, in these walls, abhorred by the world, an abomination even to brutes. Beautiful nature is shut out from me; for I am blind by day, and only when the moon sheds her wan light upon this ruin, falls the shrouding veil from mine eye."

The owl ended, and again wiped her eyes with her wing, for the narration of her wo had called forth tears. The Caliph was plunged in deep meditation by the story of the Princess. "If I am not altogether deceived," said he, "you will find that between our misfortunes a secret connection exists; but where can I find the key to this enigma?"

The owl answered him, "My lord! this also is plain to me; for once, in early youth, it was foretold to me by a wise woman, that a stork would bring me great happiness, and perhaps I might know how we may save ourselves."

The Caliph was much astonished, and inquired in what way she meant.

"The enchanter who has made us both miserable," said she, "comes once every month to these ruins. Not far from this chamber is a hall; there, with many confederates, he is wont to banquet. Already I have often watched them: they relate to one another their shameful deeds—perhaps he might then mention the magic word which you have forgotten."

"Oh, dearest Princess!" exclaimed the Caliph: "tell us—when will he come, and where is the hall?"

The owl was silent a moment, and then said: "Take it not unkindly, but only on one condition can I grant your wish."

"Speak out! speak out!" cried Chasid. "Command; whatever it may be, I am ready to obey."

"It is this: I would fain at the same time be free; this, however, can only take place, if one of you offer me his hand." At this proposition the storks seemed somewhat surprised, and the Caliph beckoned to his attendant to step aside with him a moment. "Grand-Vizier," said the Caliph before the door, "this is a stupid affair, but you can set it all right."

"Thus?" rejoined he; "that my wife, when I go home, may scratch my eyes out? Besides, I am an old man, while you are still young and unmarried, and can better give your hand to a young and beautiful princess."

"Ah! that is the point," sighed the Caliph, as he mournfully drooped his wings: "who told you she is young and fair? That is equivalent to buying a cat in a sack!" They continued to converse together for a long time, but finally, when the Caliph saw that Mansor would rather remain a stork than marry the owl, he determined sooner, himself, to accept the condition. The owl was overjoyed; she avowed to them that they could have come at no better time, since, probably, that very night, the sorcerers would assemble together.

She left the apartment with the storks, in order to lead them to the saloon; they went a long way through a gloomy passage, until at last a very bright light streamed upon them through a half-decayed wall. When they reached this place, the owl advised them to halt very quietly. From the breach, near which they were standing, they could look down upon a large saloon, adorned all around with pillars, and splendidly decorated, in which many colored lamps restored the light of day. In the midst of the saloon stood a round table, laden with various choice meats. Around the table extended a sofa, on which eight men were seated. In one of these men the storks recognised the very merchant, who had sold them the magic powder. His neighbor desired him to tell them his latest exploits; whereupon he related, among others, the story of the Caliph and his Vizier.

"What did you give them for a word?" inquired of him one of the other magicians.

"A right ponderous Latin one—Mutabor."

CHAPTER V

HEN the storks heard this through their chasm in the wall, they became almost beside themselves with joy. They ran so quickly with their long feet to the door of the ruin, that the owl could scarcely keep up with them. Thereupon spoke the Caliph to her: "Preserver of my life and that of my friend, in token of our eternal thanks for what thou hast done for us, take me as thy husband." Then he turned to the East: three times they bowed their long necks towards the sun, which was even now rising above the mountains, and at the same moment exclaimed "Mutabor!" In a twinkling they were restored, and in the excessive joy of their newly-bestowed life, alternately laughing and weeping, were folded in each other's arms. But who can describe their astonishment when they looked around? A beautiful woman, attired as a queen, stood before them. Smiling, she gave the Caliph her hand, and said, "Know you your screech-owl no longer?" It was she; the Caliph was in such transports at her beauty and pleasantness, as to cry out, that it was the most fortunate moment in his life, when he became a stork.

The three now proceeded together to Bagdad. The Caliph found in his dress, not only the box of magic powder, but also his money-bag. By means thereof, he purchased at the nearest village what was necessary for their journey, and accordingly they soon appeared before the gates of the city. Here, however, the arrival of the Caliph excited great astonishment. They had given out that he was dead, and the people were therefore highly rejoiced to have again their beloved lord.

So much the more, however, burned their hatred against the impostor Mizra. They proceeded to the palace, and caught the old magician and his son. The old man the Caliph sent to the same chamber in the ruin, which the princess, as a screech-owl, had inhabited, and there had him hung; unto the son, however, who understood nothing of his father's arts, he gave his choice,—to die, or snuff some of the powder. Having chosen the latter, the Grand-Vizier presented him the box. A hearty pinch, and the magic word of the Caliph converted him into a stork. Chasid had him locked up in an iron cage, and hung in his garden.

Long and happily lived Caliph Chasid with his spouse, the Princess; his pleasantest hours were always those, when in the afternoon the Vizier sought him; and whenever the Caliph was in a very good humor, he would let himself down so far, as to show Mansor how he looked, when a stork. He would gravely march along, with rigid feet, up and down the chamber, make a clattering noise, wave his arms like wings, and show how, in vain, he had prostrated himself to the East, and cried out, Mu—mu. To the Princess and her children, this imitation always afforded great amusement: when, however, the Caliph clattered, and bowed, and cried out, too long, then the Vizier would threaten him that he would disclose to his spouse what had been proposed outside the door of the Princess Screech-owl!

When Selim Baruch had finished his story, the merchants declared themselves delighted therewith. "Verily, the afternoon has passed away from us without our having observed it!" exclaimed one of them, throwing back the covering of the tent: "the evening wind blows cool, we can still make a good distance on our journey." To this his companions agreed; the tents were struck, and the Caravan proceeded on its way in the same order in which it had come up.

They rode almost all the night long, for it was refreshing and starry, whereas the day was sultry. At last they arrived at a convenient stopping-place; here they pitched their tents, and composed themselves to rest. To the stranger the merchants attended, as a most valued guest. One gave him cushions, a second covering, a third slaves; in a word, he was as well provided for as if he had been at home. The hottest hours of the day had already arrived, when they awoke again, and they unanimously determined to wait for evening in this place. After they had eaten together, they moved more closely to each other, and the young merchant, turning to the oldest, addressed him: "Selim Baruch yesterday made a pleasant afternoon for us; suppose Achmet, that you also tell us something, be it either from your long life, which has known so many adventures, or even a pretty

Märchen."

Upon these words Achmet was silent some time, as if he were in doubt whether to tell this or that; at last he began to speak: "Dear friends, on this our journey you have proved yourselves faithful companions, and Selim also deserves my confidence; I will therefore impart to you something of my life, of which, under other circumstances, I would speak reluctantly, and, indeed, not to any one: The History of the Spectre Ship."

THE HISTORY OF THE SPECTRE SHIP

MY father had a little shop in Balsora; he was neither rich, nor poor, but one of those who do not like to risk any thing, through fear of losing the little that they have. He brought me up plainly, but virtuously, and soon I advanced so far, that I was able to make valuable suggestions to him in his business. When I reached my eighteenth year, in the midst of his first speculation of any importance, he died; probably through anxiety at having intrusted a thousand gold pieces to the sea. I was obliged, soon after, to deem him happy in his fortunate death, for in a few weeks the intelligence reached us, that the vessel, to which my father had committed his goods, had been wrecked. This misfortune, however, could not depress my youthful spirits. I converted all that my father had left into money, and set out to try my fortune in foreign lands, accompanied only by an old servant of the family, who, on account of ancient attachment, would not part from me and my destiny.

In the harbor of Balsora we embarked, with a favorable wind. The ship, in which I had taken passage, was bound to India. We had now for fifteen days sailed in the usual track, when the Captain predicted to us a storm. He wore a thoughtful look, for it seemed he knew that, in this place, there was not sufficient depth of water to encounter a storm with safety. He ordered them to take in all sail, and we moved along quite slowly. The night set in clear and cold, and the Captain began to think that he had been mistaken in his forebodings. All at once there floated close by ours, a ship which none of us had observed before. A wild shout and cry ascended from the deck, at which, occurring at this anxious season, before a storm, I wondered not a little. But the Captain by my side was deadly pale: "My ship is lost," cried he; "there sails Death!" Before I could demand an explanation of these singular words, the sailors rushed in, weeping and wailing. "Have you seen it?" they exclaimed: "all is now over with us!"

But the Captain had words of consolation read to them out of the Koran, and seated himself at the helm. But in vain! The tempest began visibly to rise with a roaring noise, and, before an hour passed by, the ship struck and remained aground. The boats were lowered, and scarcely had the last sailors saved themselves, when the vessel went down before our eyes, and I was launched, a beggar, upon the sea. But our misfortune had still no end. Frightfully roared the tempest, the boat could no longer be governed. I fastened myself firmly to my old servant, and we mutually promised not to be separated from each other. At last the day broke, but, with the first glance of the morning-red, the wind struck and upset the boat in which we were seated. After that I saw my shipmates no more. The shock deprived me of consciousness, and when I returned to my senses, I found myself in the arms of my old faithful attendant, who had saved himself on the boat which had been upturned, and had come in search of me. The storm had abated; of our vessel there was nothing any more to be seen, but we plainly descried, at no great distance from us, another ship, towards which the waves were driving us. As we approached, I recognised the vessel as the same which had passed by us in the night, and which had thrown the Captain into such consternation. I felt a strange horror of this ship; the intimation of the Captain, which had been so fearfully corroborated, the desolate appearance of the ship, on which, although as we drew near we uttered loud cries, no one was visible, alarmed me. Nevertheless this was our only expedient; accordingly, we praised the Prophet, who had so miraculously preserved us.

From the fore-part of the ship hung down a long cable; for the purpose of laying hold of this, we paddled with our hands and feet. At last we were successful. Loudly I raised my voice, but all remained quiet as ever, on board the vessel. Then we climbed up by the rope, I, as the youngest, taking the lead. But horror! what a spectacle was there presented to my eye, as I stepped upon the deck! The floor was red with blood; upon it lay twenty or thirty corpses in Turkish costume; by the middle-mast stood a man richly attired, with sabre in hand—but his face was wan and distorted; through his forehead passed a large spike which fastened him to the mast—he was dead! Terror chained my feet; I dared hardly to breathe. At last my companion stood by my side; he, too, was overpowered at sight of the deck which exhibited no living thing, but only so many frightful corpses. After having, in the anguish of our souls, supplicated the Prophet, we ventured to move forward. At every step we looked around to see if something new, something still more horrible, would not present itself. But all remained as it was—far and wide, no living thing but ourselves, and the ocean-world. Not once did we dare to speak aloud, through fear that the dead Captain there nailed to the mast would bend his rigid eyes upon us, or lest one of the corpses should turn his head. At last we arrived at a staircase, which led into the hold. There involuntarily we came to a halt, and looked at each other, for neither of us exactly ventured to express his thoughts.

"Master," said my faithful servant, "something awful has happened here. Nevertheless, even if the ship down there below is full of murderers, still would I rather submit myself to their mercy or cruelty, than spend a longer time among these dead bodies." I agreed with him, and so we took heart, and descended, full of apprehension. But the stillness of death prevailed here also, and there was no sound save that of our steps upon the stairs. We stood before the door of the cabin; I applied my ear, and listened—there was nothing to be heard. I opened it. The room presented a confused appearance; clothes, weapons, and other articles, lay disordered together. The crew, or at least the Captain, must shortly before have been carousing, for the remains of a banquet lay scattered around. We went on from room to room, from chamber to chamber finding, in all, royal stores of silk, pearls, and other costly articles. I was beside myself with joy at the sight, for as there was no one on the ship, I thought I could appropriate all to myself; but Ibrahim thereupon called to my notice that we were still far from land, at which we could not arrive, alone and without human help.

We refreshed ourselves with the meats and drink, which we found in rich profusion, and at last ascended upon deck. But here again we shivered at the awful sight of the bodies. We determined to free ourselves therefrom, by throwing them overboard; but how were we startled to find, that no one could move them from their places! So firmly were they fastened to the floor, that to remove them one would have had to take up the planks of the deck, for which tools were wanting to us. The Captain, moreover, could not be loosened from the mast, nor could we even wrest the sabre from his rigid hand. We passed the day in sorrowful reflection on our condition; and, when night began to draw near, I gave permission to the old Ibrahim to lie down to sleep, while I would watch upon the deck, to look out for means of deliverance. When, however, the moon shone forth, and by the stars I calculated that it was about the eleventh hour, sleep so irresistibly overpowered me that I fell back, involuntarily, behind a cask which stood upon the deck. It was rather lethargy than sleep, for I plainly heard the sea beat against the side of the vessel, and the sails creak and whistle in the wind. All at once I thought I heard voices, and the steps of men upon the deck. I wished to arise and see what it was, but a strange power fettered my limbs, and I could not once open my eyes. But still more distinct became the voices; it appeared to me as if a merry crew were moving around upon the deck. In the midst of this I thought I distinguished the powerful voice of a commander, followed by the noise of ropes and sails. Gradually my senses left me; I fell into a deep slumber, in which I still seemed to hear the din of weapons, and awoke only when the sun was high in the heavens, and sent down his burning rays upon my face. Full of wonder, I gazed about me; storm, ship, the bodies, and all that I had heard in the night, recurred to me as a dream; but when I looked around, I found all as it had been the day before. Immoveable lay the bodies, immoveably was the Captain fastened to the mast; I laughed at my dream, and proceeded in search of my old companion.

The latter was seated in sorrowful meditation in the cabin. "O master," he exclaimed as I entered, "rather would I lie in the deepest bottom of the sea, than pass another night in this enchanted ship." I asked him the reason of his grief, and thus he answered me:—

"When I had slept an hour, I awoke, and heard the noise of walking to and fro over my head. I thought at first that it was you, but there were at least twenty running around; I also heard conversation and cries. At length came heavy steps upon the stairs. After this I was no longer conscious; but at times my recollection returned for a moment, and then I saw the same man who is nailed to the mast, sit down at that table, singing and drinking; and he who lies not far from him on the floor, in a scarlet cloak, sat near him, and helped him to drink." Thus spoke my old servant to me.

You may believe me, my friends, that all was not right to my mind; for there was no delusion—I too had plainly heard the dead. To sail in such company was to me horrible; my Ibrahim, however, was again absorbed in deep reflection. "I have it now!" he exclaimed at length; there occurred to him, namely, a little verse, which his grandfather, a man of experience and travel, had taught him, and which could give assistance against every ghost and spectre. He also maintained that we could, the next night, prevent the unnatural sleep which had come upon us, by repeating right fervently sentences out of the Koran.

The proposition of the old man pleased me well. In anxious expectation we saw the night set in. Near the cabin was a little room, to which we determined to retire. We bored several holes in the door, large enough to give us a view of the whole cabin; then we shut it as firmly as we could from within, and Ibrahim wrote the name of the Prophet in all four corners of the room. Thus we awaited the terrors of the night.

It might again have been about the eleventh hour, when a strong inclination for sleep began to overpower me. My companion, thereupon, advised me to repeat some sentences from the Koran, which assisted me to retain my consciousness. All at once it seemed to become lively overhead; the ropes creaked, there were steps upon the deck, and several voices were plainly distinguishable. We remained, a few moments, in intense anxiety; then we heard something descending the cabin stairs. When the old man became aware of this, he began to repeat the words which his grandfather had taught him to use against spirits and witchcraft:

"Come you, from the air descending, Rise you from the deep sea-cave, Spring you forth where flames are blending, Glide you in the dismal grave: Allah reigns, let all adore him! Own him, spirits—bow before him!"

I must confess I did not put much faith in this verse, and my hair stood on end when the door flew open. The same large, stately man entered, whom I had seen nailed to the mast. The spike still passed through the middle of his brain, but he had sheathed his sword. Behind him entered another, attired with less magnificence, whom also I had seen lying on the deck. The Captain, for he was unquestionably of this rank, had a pale countenance, a large black beard, and wildly-rolling eyes, with which he surveyed the whole apartment. I could see him distinctly, for he moved over opposite to us; but he appeared not to observe the door which concealed us. The two seated themselves at the table, which stood in the centre of the cabin, and spoke loud and fast, shouting together in an unknown tongue. They continually became more noisy and earnest, until at length, with doubled fist, the Captain brought the table a blow which shook the whole apartment. With wild laughter the other sprang up, and beckoned to the Captain to follow him. The latter rose, drew his sabre, and then both left the apartment. We breathed more freely when they were away; but our anxiety had still for a long time no end. Louder and louder became the noise upon deck; we heard hasty running to and fro, shouting, laughing, and howling. At length there came an actually hellish sound, so that we thought the deck and all the sails would fall down upon us, the clash of arms, and shrieks—of a sudden all was deep silence. When, after many hours, we ventured to go forth, we found every thing as before; not one lay differently—all were as stiff as wooden figures.

Thus passed we several days on the vessel; it moved continually towards the East, in which direction, according to my calculation, lay the land; but if by day it made many miles, by night it appeared to go back again, for we always found ourselves in the same spot when the sun went down. We could explain this in no other way, than that the dead men every night sailed back again with a full breeze. In order to prevent this, we took in all the sail before it became night, and employed the same means as at the door in the cabin; we wrote on parchment the name of the Prophet, and also, in addition, the little stanza of the grandfather, and bound them upon the furled sail. Anxiously we awaited the result in our chamber. The ghosts appeared this time not to rage so wickedly; and, mark, the next morning the sails were still rolled up as we had left them. During the day we extended only as much as was necessary to bear the ship gently along, and so in five days we made considerable headway.

At last, on the morning of the sixth day, we espied land at a short distance, and thanked Allah and his Prophet for our wonderful deliverance. This day and the following night we sailed along the coast, and on the seventh morning thought we discovered a city at no great distance: with a good deal of trouble we cast an anchor into the sea, which soon reached the bottom; then launching a boat which stood upon the deck, we rowed with all our might towards the city. After half an hour we ran into a river that emptied into the sea, and stepped ashore. At the gate we inquired what the place was called, and learned that it was an Indian city, not far from the region to which at first I had intended to sail. We repaired to a Caravansery, and refreshed ourselves after our adventurous sail. I there inquired for a wise and intelligent man, at the same time giving the landlord to understand that I would like to have one tolerably conversant with magic. He conducted me to an unsightly house in a remote street, knocked thereat, and one let me in with the injunction that I should ask only for Muley.

In the house, came to me a little old man with grizzled beard and a long nose, to demand my business. I told him I was in search of the wise Muley; he answered me that he was the man. I then asked his advice as to what I should do to the dead bodies, and how I must handle them in order to remove them from the ship.

He answered me that the people of the ship were probably enchanted on account of a crime somewhere upon the sea: he thought the spell would be dissolved by bringing them to land, but this could be done only by taking up the planks on which they lay. In the sight of God and justice, he said that the ship, together with all the goods, belonged to me, since I had, as it were, found it; and, if I would keep it very secret, and make him a small present out of my abundance, he would assist me with his slaves to remove the bodies. I promised to reward him richly, and we set out on our expedition with five slaves, who were supplied with saws and hatchets. On the way, the magician Muley could not sufficiently praise our happy expedient of binding the sails around with the sentences from the Koran. He said this was the only means, by which we could have saved ourselves.

It was still pretty early in the day when we reached the ship. We immediately set to work, and in an hour placed four in the boat. Some of the slaves were then obliged to row to land to bury them there. They told us, when they returned, that the bodies had spared them the trouble of burying, since, the moment they laid them on the earth, they had fallen to dust. We diligently set to work to saw off the bodies, and before evening all were brought to land. There were, at last, no more on board than the one that was nailed to the mast. Vainly sought we to draw the nail out of the wood, no strength was able to start it even a hair's-breadth. I knew not what next to do, for we could not hew down the mast in order to bring him to land; but in this dilemma Muley came to my assistance. He quickly ordered a slave to row to land and bring a pot of earth. When he had arrived with it, the magician pronounced over it some mysterious words, and cast it on the dead man's head. Immediately the latter opened his eyes, drew a deep breath, and the wound of the nail in his forehead began to bleed. We now drew it lightly forth, and the wounded man fell into the arms of one of the slaves.

"Who bore me hither?" he exclaimed, after he seemed to have recovered himself a little. Muley made signs to me, and I stepped up to him.

"Thank thee, unknown stranger; thou hast freed me from long torment. For fifty years has my body been sailing through these waves, and my spirit was condemned to return to it every night. But now my head has come in contact with the earth, and, my crime expiated, I can go to my fathers!"

I entreated him, thereupon, to tell how he had been brought to this horrible state, and he began—

"Fifty years ago, I was an influential, distinguished man, and resided in Algiers: a passion for gain urged me on to fit out a ship, and turn pirate. I had already followed this business some time, when once, at Zante, I took on board a Dervise, who wished to travel for nothing. I and my companions were impious men, and paid no respect to the holiness of the man; I, in particular, made sport of him. When, however, on one occasion he upbraided me with holy zeal for my wicked course of life, that same evening, after I had been drinking to excess with my pilot in the cabin, anger overpowered me. Reflecting on what the Dervise had said to me, which I would not have borne from a Sultan, I rushed upon deck, and plunged my dagger into his breast. Dying, he cursed me and my crew, and doomed us not to die and not to live, until we should lay our heads upon the earth.

"The Dervise expired, and we cast him overboard, laughing at his menaces; that same night, however, were his words fulfilled. One portion of my crew rose against me; with terrible courage the struggle continued, until my supporters fell, and I myself was nailed to the mast. The mutineers, however, also sank under their wounds, and soon my ship was but one vast grave. My eyes also closed, my breath stopped—I thought I was dying. But it was only a torpor which held me chained: the following night, at the same hour in which we had cast the Dervise into the sea, I awoke, together with all my comrades; life returned, but we could do and say nothing but what had been done and said on that fatal night. Thus we sailed for fifty years, neither living nor dying, for how could we reach the land? With mad joy we ever dashed along, with full sails, before the storm, for we hoped at last to be wrecked upon some cliff, and to compose our weary heads to rest upon the bottom of the sea; but in this we never succeeded. Now I shall die! Once again, unknown preserver, accept my thanks, and if treasures can reward thee, then take my ship in token of my gratitude."

With these words the Captain let his head drop, and expired. Like his companions, he immediately fell to dust. We collected this in a little vessel, and buried it on the shore: and I took workmen from the city to put the ship in good condition. After I had exchanged, with great advantage, the wares I had on board for others, I hired a crew, richly rewarded my friend Muley, and set sail for my fatherland. I took a circuitous route, in the course of which I landed at several islands and countries, to bring my goods to market. The Prophet blessed my undertaking. After several years I ran into Balsora, twice as rich as the dying Captain had made me. My fellow-citizens were amazed at my wealth and good fortune, and would believe nothing else but that I had found the diamond-valley of the far-famed traveller Sinbad. I left them to their belief; henceforth must the young folks of Balsora, when they have scarcely arrived at their eighteenth year, go forth into the world, like me, to seek their fortunes. I, however, live in peace and tranquillity, and every five years make a journey to Mecca, to thank the Lord for his protection, in that holy place, and to entreat for the

Captain and his crew, that He will admit them into Paradise.

The march of the Caravan proceeded the next day without hinderance, and when they halted, Selim the Stranger began thus to speak to Muley, the youngest of the merchants:

"You are, indeed, the youngest of us, nevertheless you are always in fine spirits, and, to a certainty, know for us, some right merry story. Out with it then, that it may refresh us after the heat of the day."

"I might easily tell you something," answered Muley, "which would amuse you, nevertheless modesty becomes youth in all things; therefore must my older companions have the precedence. Zaleukos is ever so grave and reserved; should not he tell us what has made his life so serious? Perhaps we could assuage his grief, if such he have; for gladly would we serve a brother, even if he belong to another creed."

The person alluded to was a Grecian merchant of middle age, handsome and strongly built, but very serious. Although he was an unbeliever, (that is, no Mussulman,) still his companions were much attached to him, for his whole conduct had inspired them with respect and confidence. He had only one hand, and some of his companions conjectured that, perhaps, this loss gave so grave a tone to his character. Zaleukos thus answered Muley's friendly request:

"I am much honored by your confidence: grief have I none, at least none from which, even with your best wishes, you can relieve me. Nevertheless, since Muley appears to blame me for my seriousness, I will relate to you something which will justify me when I am more grave than others. You see that I have lost my left hand; this came not to me at my birth, but I lost it in the most unhappy days of my life. Whether I bear the fault thereof, whether I am wrong to be more serious than my condition in life would seem to make me, you must decide, when I have told you the Story of the Hewn-off Hand."

THE STORY OF THE HEWN OFF HAND

I WAS born in Constantinople; my father was a Dragoman of the Ottoman Porte, and carried on, besides, a tolerably lucrative trade in essences and silk goods. He gave me a good education, since he partly superintended it himself, and partly had me instructed by one of our priests. At first, he intended that I should one day take charge of his business: but since I displayed greater capacity than he expected, with the advice of his friends, he resolved that I should study medicine; for a physician, if he only knows more than a common quack, can make his fortune in Constantinople.

Many Frenchmen were in the habit of coming to our house, and one of them prevailed upon my father to let me go to the city of Paris, in his fatherland, where one could learn the profession gratuitously, and with the best advantages: he himself would take me with him, at his own expense, when he returned. My father, who in his youth had also been a traveller, consented, and the Frenchman told me to hold myself in readiness in three months. I was beside myself with delight to see foreign lands, and could not wait for the moment in which we should embark. At last the stranger had finished his business, and was ready to start.

On the evening preceding our voyage, my father conducted me into his sleeping apartment; there I saw fine garments and weapons lying on the table; but what most attracted my eye was a large pile of gold, for I had never before seen so much together. My father embraced me, and said,

"See, my son, I have provided thee with garments for thy journey. These weapons are thine; they are those which thy grandfather hung upon me, when I went forth into foreign lands. I know thou canst wield them; but use them not, unless thou art attacked; then, however, lay on with right good-will. My wealth is not great; see! I have divided it into three parts: one is thine; one shall be for my support, and spare money in case of necessity; the third shall be sacred and untouched by me, it may serve thee in the hour of need." Thus spoke my old father, while tears hung in his eyes, perhaps from a presentiment, for I have never seen him since.

Our voyage was favorable; we soon reached the land of the Franks, and six days' journey brought us to the large city, Paris. Here my French friend hired me a room, and advised me to be prudent in spending my money, which amounted to two thousand thalers. In this city I lived three years, and learned all that a well-educated physician should know. I would be speaking falsely, however, if I said that I was very happy, for the customs of the people pleased me not; moreover, I had but few good friends among them, but these were young men of nobility.

The longing after my native land at length became irresistible; during the whole time I had heard nothing from my father, and I therefore seized a favorable opportunity to return home. There was going an embassy from France to the Supreme Porte: I agreed to join the train of the ambassador as surgeon, and soon arrived once more at Stamboul.

My father's dwelling, however, I found closed, and the neighbors, astonished at seeing me, said that my father had been dead for two months. The priest, who had instructed me in youth, brought me the key. Alone and forsaken, I entered the desolate house. I found all as my father had left it; but the gold which he promised to leave to me, was missing. I inquired of the priest respecting it, and he bowed and said:

"Your father died like a holy man, for he left his gold to the Church!"

This was incomprehensible to me; nevertheless, what could I do? I had no proofs against the priest, and could only congratulate myself that he had not also looked upon the house, and wares of my father, in the light of a legacy. This was the first misfortune that met me; but after this came one upon another. My reputation as a physician would not extend itself, because I was ashamed to play the quack; above all, I missed the recommendation of my father, who had introduced me to the richest and most respectable families; but now they thought no more of the poor Zaleukos. Moreover, the wares of my father found no sale, for his customers had been scattered at his death, and new ones came only after a long time. One day, as I was reflecting sorrowfully upon my situation, it occurred to me that in France I had often seen countrymen of mine, who travelled through the land, and exposed their goods at the market-places of the cities: I recollected that people gladly purchased of them, because they came from foreign lands; and that by such a trade, one could make a hundred-fold. My resolution was forthwith taken; I sold my paternal dwelling, gave a portion of the money obtained thereby to a tried friend to preserve for me, and with the remainder purchased such articles as were rare in France,—shawls, silken goods, ointments, and oils; for these I hired a place upon a vessel, and thus began my second voyage to France. It appeared as if fortune became favorable to me, the moment I had the Straits of the Dardanelles upon my back. Our voyage was short and prosperous. I travelled through the cities of France, large and small, and found, in all, ready purchasers for my goods. My friend in Stamboul continually sent me fresh supplies, and I became richer from day to day. At last when I had husbanded so well, that I believed myself able to venture on some more extensive undertaking, I went with my wares into Italy. I must, however, mention something that brought me in no little money; I called my profession also to my assistance. As soon as I arrived in a city I announced, by means of bills, that a Grecian physician was there, who had already cured many; and, truly, my balsam, and my medicines, had brought me in many a zechin.

Thus at last I reached the city of Florence, in Italy. I proposed to myself to remain longer than usual in this place, partly because it pleased me so well, partly, moreover, that I might recover from the fatigues of my journey. I hired myself a shop in the quarter of the city called St. Croce, and in a tavern not far therefrom, took a couple of fine rooms which led out upon a balcony. Immediately I had my bills carried around, which announced me as a physician and merchant. I had no sooner opened my shop than buyers streamed in upon me, and although I asked a tolerably high price, still I sold more than others, because I was attentive and friendly to my customers.

Well satisfied, I had spent four days in Florence, when one evening, after I had shut my shop, and according to custom was examining my stock of ointment-boxes, I found, in one of the smaller ones, a letter which I did not remember to have put in. I opened it and found therein an invitation to repair that night, punctually at twelve, to the bridge called the Ponte Vecchio. For some time I reflected upon this, as to who it could be that had thus invited me; as, however, I knew not a soul in Florence, I thought, as had often happened already, that one wished to lead me privately to some sick person. Accordingly I resolved to go; nevertheless, as a precautionary measure, I put on the sabre which my father had given me. As it was fast approaching midnight, I set out upon my way, and soon arrived at the Ponte Vecchio; I found the bridge forsaken and desolate, and resolved to wait until it should appear who had addressed me.

It was a cold night; the moon shone clear as I looked down upon the waters of the Arno, which sparkled in her light. On the church of the city the twelfth hour was sounding, when I looked up, and before me stood a tall man, entirely covered with a red cloak, a corner of which he held before his face. At this sudden apparition I was at first somewhat startled, but I soon recovered myself and said—

"If you have summoned me hither, tell me, what is your pleasure?"

The Red-mantle turned, and solemnly ejaculated, "Follow!"

My mind was nevertheless somewhat uneasy at the idea of going alone with this Unknown; I stood still and said, "Not so, dear sir; you will first tell me whither; moreover, you may show me your face a little, that I may see whether you have good intentions towards me."

The Stranger, however, appeared not to be concerned thereat. "If thou wishest it not, Zaleukos, then remain!" answered he, moving away. At this my anger burned.

"Think you," I cried, "that I will suffer a man to play the fool with me, and wait here this cold night for nothing?" In three bounds I reached him; crying still louder, I seized him by the cloak, laying the other hand upon my sabre; but the mantle remained in my hand, and the Unknown vanished around the nearest corner. My anger gradually cooled; I still had the cloak, and this should furnish the key to this strange adventure. I put it on, and moved towards home. Before I had taken a hundred steps, somebody passed very near, and whispered in the French tongue, "Observe, Count, to-night, we can do nothing." Before I could look around, this somebody had passed, and I saw only a shadow hovering near the houses. That this exclamation was addressed to the mantle, and not to me, I plainly perceived; nevertheless, this threw no light upon the matter. Next morning I considered what was best to be done. At first I thought of having proclamation made respecting the cloak, that I had found it; but in that case the Unknown could send for it by a third person, and I would have no explanation of the matter. While thus meditating I took a nearer view of the garment. It was of heavy Genoese velvet, of dark red color, bordered with fur from Astrachan, and richly embroidered with gold. The gorgeousness of the cloak suggested to me a plan, which I resolved to put in execution. I carried it to my shop and offered it for sale, taking care, however, to set so high a price upon it, that I would be certain to find no purchaser. My object in this was to fix my eye keenly upon every one who should come to inquire after it; for the figure of the Unknown, which, after the loss of the mantle, had been exposed to me distinctly though transiently, I could recognise out of thousands. Many merchants came after the cloak, the extraordinary beauty of which drew all eyes upon it; but none bore the slightest resemblance to the Unknown, none would give for it the high price of two hundred zechins. It was surprising to me, that when I asked one and another whether there was a similar mantle in Florence, all answered in the negative, and protested that they had never seen such costly and elegant workmanship.

It was just becoming evening, when at last there came a young man who had often been in there, and had also that very day bid high for the mantle; he threw upon the table a bag of zechins, exclaiming—

"By Heaven! Zaleukos, I must have your mantle, should I be made a beggar by it." Immediately he began to count out his gold pieces. I was in a great dilemma; I had exposed the mantle, in order thereby to get a sight of my unknown friend, and now came a young simpleton to give the unheard-of price. Nevertheless, what remained for me? I complied, for on the other hand the reflection consoled me, that my night adventure would be so well rewarded. The young man put on the cloak and departed; he turned, however, upon the threshold, while he loosened a paper which was attached to the collar, and threw it towards me, saying, "Here, Zaleukos, hangs something, that does not properly belong to my purchase." Indifferently, I received the note; but lo! these were the contents:—

"This night, at the hour thou knowest, bring the mantle to the Ponte Vecchio; four hundred zechins await thee!"

I stood as one thunder-struck: thus had I trifled with fortune, and entirely missed my aim. Nevertheless, I reflected not long; catching up the two hundred zechins, I bounded to the side of the young man and said, "Take your zechins again, my good friend, and leave me the cloak; I cannot possibly part with it."

At first he treated the thing as a jest, but when he saw it was earnest, he fell in a passion at my presumption, and called me a fool; and thus at last we came to blows. I was fortunate enough to seize the mantle in the scuffle, and was already making off with it, when the young man called the police to his assistance, and had both of us carried before a court of justice. The magistrate was much astonished at the accusation, and adjudged the cloak to my opponent. I however, offered the young man twenty, fifty, eighty, at last a hundred, zechins, in addition to his two hundred, if he would surrender it to me. What my entreaties could not accomplish, my gold did. He took my good zechins, while I went off in triumph with the mantle, obliged to be satisfied with being taken for a madman by every one in Florence. Nevertheless, the opinion of the people was a matter of indifference to me, for I knew better than they, that I would still gain by the bargain.

With impatience I awaited the night; at the same hour as the preceding day, I proceeded to the Ponte Vecchio, the mantle under my arm. With the last stroke of the clock, came the figure out of darkness to my side: beyond a doubt it was the man of the night before.

"Hast thou the cloak?" I was asked.

"Yes, sir," I replied, "but it cost me a hundred zechins cash."

"I know it," rejoined he; "look, here are four hundred." He moved with me to the broad railing of the bridge and counted out the gold pieces; brightly they glimmered in the moonshine, their lustre delighted my heart—ah! it did not foresee that this was to be its last joy. I put the money in my pocket, and then wished to get a good view of the generous stranger, but he had a mask before his face, through which two dark eyes frightfully beamed upon me.

"I thank you, sir, for your kindness," said I to him; "what further desire you of me? I told you before, however, that it must be nothing evil."

"Unnecessary trouble," answered he, throwing the cloak over his shoulders; "I needed your assistance as a physician, nevertheless not for a living, but for a dead person."

"How can that be?" exclaimed I in amazement.

"I came with my sister from a distant land," rejoined he, at the same time motioning me to follow him, "and took up my abode with a friend of our family. A sudden disease carried off my sister yesterday, and our relations wished to bury her this morning. According to an old usage of our family, however, all are to repose in the sepulchre of our fathers; many who have died in foreign lands, nevertheless sleep there embalmed. To my relations now I grant the body, but to my father must I bring at least the head of his daughter, that he may see it once again."

In this custom of severing the head from near relatives there was to me, indeed, something awful; nevertheless, I ventured to say nothing against it, through fear of offending the Unknown. I told him, therefore, that I was well acquainted with the art of embalming the dead, and asked him to lead me to the body. Notwithstanding, I could not keep myself from inquiring why all this must be done so secretly in the night. He answered me that his relations, who considered his purpose inhuman, would prevent him from accomplishing it by day; but only let the head once be cut off, and they could say little more about it: he could, indeed, have brought the head to me, but a natural feeling prevented him from cutting it off himself.

These words brought us to a large splendid house; my companion pointed it out to me as the termination of our nocturnal walk. We passed the principal door, and entering a small gate, which the stranger carefully closed after him, ascended, in the dark, a narrow, winding staircase. This brought us to a dimly-lighted corridor, from which we entered an apartment; a lamp, suspended from the ceiling, shed its brilliant rays around.

In this chamber stood a bed, on which lay the corpse; the Unknown turned away his face, as if wishing to conceal his tears. He beckoned me to the bed, and bidding me set about my business speedily yet carefully, went out by the door.

I seized my knives, which, as a physician, I constantly carried with me, and approached the bed. Only the head of the corpse was visible, but that was so beautiful that the deepest compassion involuntarily came over me. In long braids the dark hair hung down; the face was pale, the eyes closed. At first, I made an incision in the skin, according to the practice of surgeons when they remove a limb. Then I took my sharpest knife and cut entirely through the throat. But, horror! the dead opened her eyes—shut them again—and in a deep sigh seemed now, for the first time, to breathe forth her life! Straightway a stream of hot blood sprang forth from the wound. I was convinced that I had killed the poor girl; for that she was dead there could be no doubt—from such a wound there was no chance of recovering. I stood some moments in anxious wo, thinking on what had happened. Had the Red-mantle deceived me, or was his sister, perhaps, only apparently dead? The latter appeared to me more probable. Yet I dared not tell the brother of the deceased, that, perhaps, a less rash blow would have aroused, without having killed her; therefore I began to sever the head entirely—but once again the dying one groaned, stretched herself out in a convulsion of pain, and breathed her last. Then terror overpowered me, and I rushed shivering out of the apartment.

But outside in the corridor it was dark, for the lamp had died out; no trace of my companion was perceptible, and I was obliged to move along by the wall, at hazard in the dark, in order to reach the winding-stairs. I found them at last, and descended, half falling, half gliding. There was no one below; the door was only latched, and I breathed more freely when I was in the street, out of the uneasy atmosphere of the house. Spurred on by fear, I ran to my dwelling, and buried myself in the pillow of my bed, in order to forget the horrid crime I had committed. But sleep fled my eyelids, and soon morning admonished me again to collect myself. It seemed probable to me, that the man who had led me to this villainous deed, as it now appeared to me, would not denounce me. I immediately resolved to attend to my business in my shop, and to put on as careless an air as possible. But, alas! a new misfortune, which I now for the first time observed, augmented my sorrow. My cap and girdle, as also my knives, were missing; and I knew not whether they had been left in the chamber of the dead, or lost during my flight. Alas! the former seemed more probable, and they could discover in me the murderer.

I opened my shop at the usual time; a neighbor stepped in, as was his custom, being a communicative man. "Ah! what say you to the horrid deed," he cried, "that was committed last night?" I started as if I knew nothing. "How! know you not that with which the whole city is filled? Know you not that last night, the fairest flower in Florence, Bianca, the daughter of the Governor, was murdered? Ah! only yesterday I saw her walking happily through the streets with her bridegroom, for to-day she would have had her nuptial festival!"

Every word of my neighbor was a dagger to my heart; and how often returned my torments! for each of my customers told me the story, one more frightfully than another; yet not one could tell it half so horribly as it had seemed to me. About mid-day, an officer of justice unexpectedly walked into my shop, and asked me to clear it of the bystanders.

"Signor Zaleukos," said he, showing me the articles I had lost, "belong these things to you?" I reflected whether I should not entirely disown them; but when I saw through the half-opened door, my landlord and several acquaintances, who could readily testify against me, I determined not to make the matter worse by a falsehood, and acknowledged the articles exhibited as my own. The officer told me to follow him, and conducted me to a spacious building, which I soon recognised as the prison. Then, a little farther on, he showed me into an apartment.

My situation was terrible, as I reflected on it in my solitude. The thought of having committed a murder, even against my wish, returned again and again. Moreover, I could not conceal from myself that the glance of the gold had dazzled my senses; otherwise I would not have fallen so blindly into the snare.

Two hours after my arrest, I was led from my chamber, and after descending several flights of stairs, entered a spacious saloon. Around a long table hung with black, were seated twelve men, mostly gray with age. Along the side of the room, benches were arranged, on which were seated the first people of Florence. In the gallery, which was built quite high, stood the spectators, closely crowded together. As soon as I reached the black table, a man with a gloomy, sorrowful air arose—it was the Governor. He told the audience that, as a father, he could not judge impartially in this matter, and that he, for this occasion, would surrender his seat to the oldest of the senators. The latter was a gray-headed man, of at least ninety years. He arose, stooping beneath the weight of age; his temples were covered with thin white hair, but his eyes still burned brightly, and his voice was strong and steady. He began by asking me whether I confessed the murder. I entreated his attention, and with dauntless, distinct voice, related what I had done and all that I knew. I observed that the Governor during my recital turned first pale, then red, and when I concluded, became furious. "How, wretch!" he cried out to me, "wishest thou thus to lay upon another, the crime thy avarice has committed?"

The Senator rebuked him for his interruption, after having of his own free will resigned his right; moreover, that it was not so clear, that I had done the deed through avarice, for according to his own testimony, nothing had been taken from the corpse. Yes, he went still further; he told the Governor that he must give an account of his daughter's early life, for in this way only could one conclude whether I had told the truth or not. Immediately he closed the court for that day, for the purpose, as he said, of consulting the papers of the deceased, which the Governor was to give him. I was carried back to my prison, where I passed a sorrowful day, constantly occupied with the ardent hope, that they would in some way discover the connection between the deceased and the Red-mantle.

Full of hope, I proceeded the next day to the justice-hall. Several letters lay upon the table; the old Senator asked whether they were of my writing. I looked at them, and found that they were by the same hand as both the letters that I had received. This I disclosed to the Senator; but he seemed to give but little weight to it, answering that I must have written both, for the name subscribed was unquestionably a Z, the initial of my name. The letters, however, contained menaces against the deceased, and warnings against the marriage which she was on the point of consummating. The Governor seemed to have imparted something strange and untrue, with respect to my person; for I was treated this day with more suspicion and severity. For my justification, I appealed to the papers, which would be found in my room, but I was informed that search had been made and nothing found. Thus, at the close of the court, vanished all my hope; and when, on the third day, I was led again to the hall, the judgment was read aloud, that I was convicted of a premeditated murder, and sentenced to death. To such extremity had I come; forsaken by all that was dear to me on earth, far from my native land, innocent and in the bloom of my years, I was to die by the axe!

On the evening of this terrible day which had decided my fate, I was seated in my lonely dungeon, my hopes past, my thoughts seriously turned upon death, when the door of my prison opened, and a man entered who regarded me long in silence.

"Do I see you again, in this situation, Zaleukos?" he began. By the dim light of my lamp I had not recognised him, but the sound of his voice awoke within me old recollections. It was Valetty, one of the few friends I had made during my studies at Paris. He said that he had casually come to Florence, where his father, a distinguished man, resided; he had heard of my story, and come to see me once more, to inquire with his own lips, how I could have been guilty of such an awful crime. I told him the whole history: he seemed lost in wonder, and conjured me to tell him, my only friend, all the truth, and not to depart with a lie upon my tongue. I swore to him with the most solemn oath, that I had spoken the truth; and that no other guilt could be attached to me, than that, having been blinded by the glance of the gold, I had not seen the improbability of the Stranger's story. "Then did you not know Bianca?" asked he. I assured him that I had never seen her. Valetty thereupon told me that there was a deep mystery in the matter; that the Governor in great haste had urged my condemnation, and that a report was current among the people, that I had known Bianca for a long time, and had murdered her out of revenge for her intended marriage with another. I informed him that all this was probably true of the Red-mantle, but that I could not prove his participation in the deed. Valetty embraced me, weeping, and promised me to do all that he could; to save my life, if nothing more.

I had not much hope; nevertheless, I knew that my friend was a wise man, and well acquainted with the laws, and that he would do all in his power to preserve me.

Two long days was I in suspense; at length Valetty appeared. "I bring consolation, though even that is attended with sorrow. You shall live and be free, but with the loss of a hand!"

Overjoyed, I thanked my friend for my life. He told me that the Governor had been inexorable, and would not once look into the matter: that at length, however, rather than appear unjust, he had agreed, if a similar case could be found in the annals of Florentine history, that my penalty should be regulated by the punishment that was then inflicted. He and his father had searched, day and night, in the old books, and had at length found a case similar in every respect to mine; the sentence there ran thus:—

"He shall have his left hand cut off; his goods shall be confiscated, and he himself banished forever!"

Such now was my sentence, also, and I was to prepare for the painful hour that awaited me. I will not bring before your eyes the frightful moment, in which, at the open market-place, I laid my hand upon the block; in which my own blood in thick streams flowed over me!

Valetty took me to his house until I had recovered, and then generously supplied me with money for my journey, for all that I had so laboriously acquired was confiscated to Justice. I went from Florence to Sicily, and thence, by the first ship I could find, to Constantinople. My hopes, which rested on the sum of money I had left with my friend, were not disappointed. I proposed that I should live with him—how astonished was I, when he asked why I occupied not my own house! He told me that a strange man had, in my name, bought a house in the quarter of the Greeks, and told the neighbors that I would soon, myself, return. I immediately proceeded to it with my friend, and was joyfully received by all my old acquaintances. An aged merchant handed me a letter which the man who purchased for me had left. I read:—

"Zaleukos! two hands stand ready to work unceasingly, that thou mayest not feel the loss of one. That house which thou seest and all therein are thine, and every year shalt thou receive so much, that thou shalt be among the rich of thy nation. Mayest thou forgive one who is more unhappy than thyself!"

I could guess who was the writer, and the merchant told me, in answer to my inquiry that it was a man covered with a red cloak, whom he had taken for a Frenchman. I knew enough to convince me that the Unknown was not entirely devoid of generous feeling. In my new house I found all arranged in the best style; a shop, moreover, full of wares, finer than any I had ever had. Ten years have elapsed since then; more in compliance with ancient custom, than because it is necessary, do I continue to travel in foreign lands for purposes of trade, but the land which was so fatal to me I have never seen since. Every year I receive a thousand pieces of gold; but although it rejoices me to know that this Unfortunate is so noble, still can his money never remove wo from my soul, for there lives forever the heart-rending image of the murdered Bianca!

Thus ended the story of Zaleukos, the Grecian merchant. With great interest had the others listened; the stranger, in particular, seemed to be wrapt up in it: more than once he had drawn a deep sigh, and Muley looked as if he had had tears in his eyes. No one spoke for some time after the recital.

"And hate you not the Unknown, who so basely cost you a noble member of your body, and even put your life in danger?" inquired Selim.

"Perhaps there were hours at first," answered the Greek, "in which my heart accused him before God, of having brought this misfortune upon me, and embittered my life; but I found consolation in the religion of my fathers, which commanded me to love my enemies. Moreover, he probably is more unhappy than myself."

"You are a noble man!" exclaimed Selim, cordially pressing the hand of the Greek.

The leader of the escort, however, here interrupted their conversation. He came with a troubled air into the tent, and told them that they could not give themselves up to repose, for this was the place in which Caravans were usually attacked, and his guards imagined they had seen several horsemen in the distance.

The merchants were confounded at this intelligence. Selim, the stranger, however, expressed wonder at their alarm, saying they were so well escorted they need not fear a troop of Arabian robbers.

"Yes, sir," rejoined to him the leader of the guard; "were he only a common outlaw, we could compose ourselves to rest without anxiety; but for some time back, the frightful Orbasan has shown himself again, and it is well to be upon our guard."

The stranger inquired who this Orbasan was, and Achmet, the old merchant, answered him:—

"Various rumors are current among the people with respect to this wonderful man. Some hold him to be a supernatural being, because, with only five or six men, he has frequently fallen upon a whole encampment; others regard him as a bold Frenchman, whom misfortune has driven into this region: out of all this, however, thus much alone is certain, that he is an abandoned robber and highwayman."

"That can you not prove," answered Lezah, one of the merchants. "Robber as he is, he is still a noble man, and such has he shown himself to my brother, as I can relate to you. He has formed his whole band of well-disciplined men, and as long as he marches through the desert, no other band ventures to show itself. Moreover, he robs not as others, but only exacts a tribute from the caravans; whoever willingly pays this, proceeds without further danger, for Orbasan is lord of the wilderness!"

Thus did the travellers converse together in the tent; the guards, however, who were stationed around the resting-place, began to become uneasy. A tolerably large band of armed horsemen showed themselves at the distance of half a league. They appeared to be riding straight to the encampment; one of the guard came into the tent, to inform them that they would probably be attacked.

The merchants consulted among themselves as to what they should do, whether to march against them, or await the attack. Achmet and the two elder merchants inclined to the latter course; the fiery Muley, however, and Zaleukos desired the former, and summoned the stranger to their assistance. He, however, quietly drew forth from his girdle a little blue cloth spangled with red stars, bound it upon a lance, and commanded one of the slaves to plant it in front of the tent: he would venture his life upon it, he said, that the horsemen, when they saw this signal, would quietly march back again. Muley trusted not the result; still the slave put out the lance in front of the tent. Meanwhile all in the camp had seized their weapons, and were looking upon the horsemen in eager expectation. The latter, however, appeared to have espied the signal; they suddenly swerved from their direct course towards the encampment, and, in a large circle, moved off to the side.

Struck with wonder, the travellers stood some moments, gazing alternately at the horsemen and the stranger. The latter stood in front of the tent quite indifferently, as though nothing had happened, looking upon the plain before him. At last Muley broke the silence.

"Who art thou, mighty stranger," he exclaimed, "that restrainest with a glance the wild hordes of the desert?"

"You rate my art higher than it deserves," answered Selim Baruch. "I observed this signal when I fled from captivity; what it means, I know not—only this much I know, that whoever travels with this sign, is under great protection."

The merchants thanked the stranger, and called him their preserver; indeed, the number of the robbers was so great, that the Caravan could not, probably, for any length of time, have offered an effectual resistance.

With lighter hearts they now gave themselves to sleep; and

when the sun began to sink, and the evening wind to pass over the sand-plain, they struck their tents, and marched on. The next day they halted safely, only one day's journey from the entrance of the desert. When the travellers had once more collected in the large tent, Lezah, the merchant, took up the discourse.

"I told you, yesterday, that the dreaded Orbasan was a noble man; permit me to prove it to you, to-day, by the relation of my brother's adventure. My father was Cadi of Acara. He had three children; I was the eldest, my brother and sister being much younger than myself. When I was twenty years old, a brother of my father took me under his protection; he made me heir to his property, on condition that I should remain with him until his death. He however had reached an old age, so that before two years I returned to my native land, having known nothing, before, of the misfortune which had meanwhile fallen upon my family, and how Allah had turned it to advantage."

FATIMA'S

DELIVERANCE.

FATIMA'S DELIVERANCE

MY brother Mustapha and my sister Fatima were almost of the same age; the former was at most but two years older. They loved each other fervently, and did in concert, all that could lighten, for our suffering father, the burden of his old age. On Fatima's seventeenth birthday, my brother prepared a festival. He invited all her companions, and set before them a choice banquet in the gardens of our father, and, towards evening, proposed to them to take a little sail upon the sea, in a boat which he had hired, and adorned in grand style. Fatima and her companions agreed with joy, for the evening was fine, and the city, particularly when viewed by evening from the sea, promised a magnificent prospect. The girls, however, were so well pleased upon the bark, that they continually entreated my brother to go farther out upon the sea. Mustapha, however, yielded reluctantly, because a Corsair had been seen, for several days back, in that vicinity.

Not far from the city, a promontory projected into the sea; thither the maidens were anxious to go, in order to see the sun sink into the water. Having rowed thither, they beheld a boat occupied by armed men. Anticipating no good, my brother commanded the oarsmen to turn the vessel, and make for land. His apprehensions seemed, indeed, to be confirmed, for the boat quickly approached that of my brother, and getting ahead of it, (for it had more rowers,) ran between it and the land. The young girls, moreover, when they knew the danger to which they were exposed, sprang up with cries and lamentations: in vain Mustapha sought to quiet them, in vain enjoined upon them to be still, lest their running to and fro should upset the vessel. It was of no avail; and when, in consequence of the proximity of the other boat, all ran upon the further side, it was upset.

Meanwhile, they had observed from the land the approach of the strange boat, and, inasmuch as, for some time back, they had been in anxiety on account of Corsairs, their suspicions were excited, and several boats put off from the land to their assistance: but they only came in time to pick up the drowning. In the confusion, the hostile boat escaped. In both barks, however, which had taken in those who were preserved, they were uncertain whether all had been saved. They approached each other, and, alas! found that my sister and one of her companions were missing; at the same time, in their number a stranger was discovered, who was known to none. In answer to Mustapha's threats, he confessed that he belonged to the hostile ship, which was lying at anchor two miles to the eastward, and that his companions had left him behind in their hasty flight, while he was engaged in assisting to pick up the maidens; moreover, he said he had seen two taken on board their boat.

The grief of my old father was without bounds, but Mustapha also was afflicted unto death, for not only had his beloved sister been lost, and did he accuse himself of having been the cause of her misfortune, but, also, her companion who had shared it with her, had been promised to him by her parents as his wife; still had he not dared to avow it to our father, because her family was poor, and of low descent. My father, however, was a stern man; as soon as his sorrow had subsided a little, he called Mustapha before him, and thus spake to him:—

"Thy folly has deprived me of the consolation of my old age, and the joy of my eyes. Go! I banish thee forever from my sight! I curse thee and thine offspring—and only when thou shalt restore to me my Fatima, shall thy head be entirely free from a father's execrations!"

This my poor brother had not expected; already, before this, he had determined to go in search of his sister and her friend, after having asked the blessing of his father upon his efforts, and now that father had sent him forth into the world, laden with his curse. As, however, his former grief had bowed him down, so this consummation of misfortune, which he had not deserved, tended to steel his mind. He went to the imprisoned pirate, and, demanding whither the ship was bound, learned that she carried on a trade in slaves, and usually had a great sale thereof in Balsora.

On his return to the house, in order to prepare for his journey, the anger of his father seemed to have subsided a little, for he sent him a purse full of gold, to support him during his travels. Mustapha, thereupon, in tears took leave of the parents of Zoraida, (for so his affianced was called,) and set out upon the route to Balsora.

Mustapha travelled by land, because from our little city there was no ship that went direct to Balsora. He was obliged, therefore, to use all expedition, in order not to arrive too long after the sea-robbers. Having a good horse and no luggage, he hoped to reach this city by the end of the sixth day. On the evening of the fourth, however, as he was riding all alone upon his way, three men came suddenly upon him. Having observed that they were well-armed and powerful men, and sought his money and his horse, rather than his life, he cried out that he would yield himself to them. They dismounted, and tied his feet together under his horse; then they placed him in their midst, and, without a word spoken, trotted quickly away with him; one of them having seized his bridle.

Mustapha gave himself up to a feeling of gloomy despair; the curse of his father seemed already to be undergoing its accomplishment on the unfortunate one, and how could he hope to save his sister and Zoraida, should he, robbed of all his means, even be able to devote his poor life to their deliverance? Mustapha and his silent companions might have ridden about an hour, when they entered a little valley. The vale was enclosed by lofty trees; a soft, dark-green turf, and a stream which ran swiftly through its midst, invited to repose. In this place were pitched from fifteen to twenty tents, to the stakes of which were fastened camels and fine horses: from one of these tents distinctly sounded the melody of a guitar, blended with two fine manly voices. It seemed to my brother as if people who had chosen so blithesome a resting-place, could have no evil intentions towards himself; and accordingly, without apprehension, he obeyed the summons of his conductors, who had unbound his feet, and made signs to him to follow. They led him into a tent which was larger than the rest, and on the inside was magnificently fitted up. Splendid cushions embroidered with gold, woven carpets, gilded censers, would elsewhere have bespoken opulence and respectability, but here seemed only the booty of a robber band. Upon one of the cushions an old and small-sized man was reclining: his countenance was ugly; a dark-brown and shining skin, a disgusting expression around his eyes, and a mouth of malicious cunning, combined to render his whole appearance odious. Although this man sought to put on a commanding air, still Mustapha soon perceived that not for him was the tent so richly adorned, and the conversation of his conductors seemed to confirm him in his opinion.

"Where is the Mighty?" inquired they of the little man.

"He is out upon a short hunt," was the answer; "but he has commissioned me to attend to his affairs."

"That has he not wisely done," rejoined one of the robbers; "for it must soon be determined whether this dog is to die or be ransomed, and that the Mighty knows better than thou."

Being very sensitive in all that related to his usurped dignity, the little man, raising himself, stretched forward in order to reach the other's ear with the extremity of his hand, for he seemed desirous of revenging himself by a blow; but when he saw that his attempt was fruitless, he set about abusing him (and indeed the others did not remain much in his debt) to such a degree, that the tent resounded with their strife. Thereupon, of a sudden, the tent-door opened, and in walked a tall, stately man, young and handsome as a Persian prince. His garments and weapons, with the exception of a richly-mounted poniard and gleaming sabre, were plain and simple; his serious eye, however, and his whole appearance, demanded respect without exciting fear.

"Who is it that dares to engage in strife within my tent?" exclaimed he, as they started back aghast. For a long time deep stillness prevailed, till at last one of those who had captured Mustapha, related to him how it had begun. Thereupon the countenance of "the Mighty," as they had called him, seemed to grow red with passion.

"When would I have placed thee, Hassan, over my concerns?" he cried, in frightful accents, to the little man. The latter, in his fear, shrunk until he seemed even smaller than before, and crept towards the door of the tent. One step of the Mighty was sufficient to send him through the entrance with a long singular bound. As soon as the little man had vanished, the three led Mustapha before the master of the tent, who had meanwhile reclined upon the cushion.

"Here bring we thee him, whom thou commandedst us to take." He regarded the prisoner for some time, and then said, "Bashaw of Sulieika, thine own conscience will tell thee why thou standest before Orbasan." When my brother heard this, he bowed low and answered:—

"My lord, you appear to labor under a mistake; I am a poor unfortunate, not the Bashaw, whom you seek." At this all were amazed; the master of the tent, however, said:—

"Dissimulation can help you little, for I will summon the people who know you well." He commanded them to bring in Zuleima. An old woman was led into the tent, who, on being asked whether in my brother she recognised the Bashaw of Sulieika, answered:—

"Yes, verily! And I swear by the grave of the Prophet, it is the Bashaw, and no other!"

"Seest thou, wretch, that thy dissimulation has become as water?" cried out the Mighty in a furious tone. "Thou art too pitiful for me to stain my good dagger with thy blood, but to-morrow, when the sun is up, will I bind thee to the tail of my horse, and gallop with thee through the woods, until they separate behind the hills of Sulieika!" Then sank my poor brother's courage within him.

"It is my cruel father's curse, that urges me to an ignominious death," exclaimed he, weeping; "and thou, too, art lost, sweet sister, and thou, Zoraida!"

"Thy dissimulation helps thee not," said one of the robbers, as he bound his hands behind his back. "Come, out of the tent with thee! for the Mighty is biting his lips, and feeling for his dagger. If thou wouldst live another night, bestir thyself!"

Just as the robbers were leading my brother from the tent, they met three of their companions, who were also pushing a captive before them. They entered with him. "Here bring we the Bashaw, as thou hast commanded," said they, conducting the prisoner before the cushion of the Mighty. While they were so doing, my brother had an opportunity of examining him, and was struck with surprise at the remarkable resemblance which this man bore to himself; the only difference being, that he was of more gloomy aspect, and had a black beard. The Mighty seemed much astonished at the resemblance of the two captives.

"Which of you is the right one?" he asked, looking alternately at Mustapha and the other.

"If thou meanest the Bashaw of Sulieika," answered the latter in a haughty tone, "I am he!"

The Mighty regarded him for a long time with his grave, terrible eye, and then silently motioned to them to lead him off. This having been done, he approached my brother, severed his bonds with his dagger, and invited him by signs to sit upon the cushion beside him. "It grieves me, stranger," he said, "that I took you for this villain. It has happened, however, by some mysterious interposition of Providence, which placed you in the hands of my companions, at the very hour in which the destruction of this wretch was ordained."

Mustapha, thereupon, entreated him only for permission to pursue his journey immediately, for this delay might cost him much. The Mighty asked what business it could be that required such haste, and, when Mustapha had told him all, he persuaded him to spend that night in his tent, and allow his horse some rest; and promised the next morning to show him a route which would bring him to Balsora in a day and a half. My brother consented, was sumptuously entertained, and slept soundly till morning in the robber's tent.

Upon awaking, he found himself all alone in the tent, but, before the entrance, heard several voices in conversation, which seemed to belong to the swarthy little man and the bandit-chief. He listened awhile, and to his horror heard the little man eagerly urging the other to slay the stranger, since, if he were let go, he could betray them all. Mustapha immediately perceived that the little man hated him, for having been the cause of his rough treatment the day before. The Mighty seemed to be reflecting a moment.

"No," said he; "he is my guest, and the laws of hospitality are with me sacred: moreover, he does not look like one that would betray us."

Having thus spoken, he threw back the tent-cover, and walked in. "Peace be with thee, Mustapha!" he said: "let us taste the morning-drink, and then prepare thyself for thy journey." He offered my brother a cup of sherbet, and after they had drunk, they saddled their horses, and Mustapha mounted, with a lighter heart, indeed, than when he entered the vale. They had soon turned their backs upon the tents, and took a broad path, which led into the forest. The Mighty informed my brother, that this Bashaw whom they had captured in the chase, had promised them that they should remain undisturbed within his jurisdiction; but some weeks before, he had taken one of their bravest men, and had him hung, after the most terrible tortures. He had waited for him a long time, and to-day he must die. Mustapha ventured not to say a word in opposition, for he was glad to have escaped himself with a whole skin.

At the entrance of the forest, the Mighty checked his horse, showed Mustapha the way, and gave him his hand with these words: "Mustapha, thou becamest in a strange way the guest of the robber Orbasan. I will not ask thee not to betray what thou hast seen and heard. Thou hast unjustly endured the pains of death, and I owe thee a recompense. Take this dagger as a remembrance, and when thou hast need of help, send it to me, and I will hasten to thy assistance. This purse thou wilt perhaps need upon thy journey."

My brother thanked him for his generosity; he took the dagger, but refused the purse. Orbasan, however, pressed once again his hand, let the money fall to the ground, and galloped with the speed of the wind into the forest. Mustapha, seeing that he could not overtake him, dismounted to secure the purse, and was astonished at the great magnanimity of his host, for it contained a large sum of gold. He thanked Allah for his deliverance, commended the generous robber to his mercy, and again started, with fresh courage, upon the route to Balsora.

Lezah paused, and looked inquiringly at Achmet, the old merchant.

"No! if it be so," said the latter, "then will I gladly correct my opinion of Orbasan; for indeed he acted nobly towards thy brother."

"He behaved like a brave Mussulman," exclaimed Muley; "but I hope thou hast not here finished thy story, for, as it seems to me, we are all eager to hear still further, how it went with thy brother, and whether he succeeded in rescuing thy sister and the fair Zoraida."

"I will willingly proceed," rejoined Lezah, "if it be not tiresome to you; for my brother's history is, throughout, full of the most wonderful adventures."

About the middle of the seventh day after his departure, Mustapha entered the gate of Balsora. As soon as he had arrived at a caravansery, he inquired whether the slave-market, which was held here every year, had opened; but received the startling answer, that he had come two days too late. His informer deplored his tardiness, telling him that on the last day of the market, two female slaves had arrived, of such great beauty as to attract to themselves the eyes of all the merchants.

He inquired more particularly as to their appearance, and there was no doubt in his mind, that they were the unfortunate ones of whom he was in search. Moreover, he learned that the man who had purchased them both, was called Thiuli-Kos, and lived forty leagues from Balsora, an illustrious and wealthy, but quite old man, who had been in his early years Capudan-Bashaw of the Sultan, but had now settled down into private life with the riches he had acquired.

Mustapha was, at first, on the point of remounting his horse with all possible speed, in order to overtake Thiuli-Kos, who could scarcely have had a day's start; but when he reflected that, as a single man, he could not prevail against the powerful traveller, could still less rescue from him his prey, he set about reflecting for another plan, and soon hit upon one. His resemblance to the Bashaw of Sulieika, which had almost been fatal to him, suggested to him the thought of going to the house of Thiuli-Kos under this name, and, in that way, making an attempt for the deliverance of the two unfortunate maidens. Accordingly he hired attendants and horses, in which the money of Orbasan opportunely came to his assistance, furnished himself and his servants with splendid garments, and set out in the direction of Thiuli's castle. After five days he arrived in its vicinity. It was situated in a beautiful plain, and was surrounded on all sides by lofty walls, which were but slightly overtopped by the structure itself. When Mustapha had arrived quite near, he dyed his hair and beard black, and stained his face with the juice of a plant, which gave it a brownish color, exactly similar to that of the Bashaw. From this place he sent forward one of his attendants to the castle, and bade him ask a night's lodging, in the name of the Bashaw of Sulieika. The servant soon returned in company with four finely-attired slaves, who took Mustapha's horse by the bridle, and led him into the court-yard. There they assisted him to dismount, and four others escorted him up a wide marble staircase, into the presence of Thiuli.

The latter personage, an old, robust man, received my brother respectfully, and had set before him the best that his castle could afford. After the meal, Mustapha gradually turned the conversation upon the new slaves; whereupon, Thiuli praised their beauty, but expressed regret because they were so sorrowful; nevertheless he believed that would go over after a time. My brother was much delighted at his reception, and, with hope beating high in his bosom, lay down to rest.

He might, perhaps, have been sleeping an hour, when he was awakened by the rays of a lamp, which fell dazzlingly upon his eyes. When he had raised himself up, he believed himself dreaming, for there before him stood the very same little, swarthy fellow of Orbasan's tent, a lamp in his hand, his wide mouth distended with a disgusting laugh. Mustapha pinched himself in the arm, and pulled his nose, in order to see if he were really awake, but the figure remained as before.

"What wishest thou by my bed?" exclaimed Mustapha, recovering from his amazement.

"Do not disquiet yourself so much, my friend," answered the little man. "I made a good guess as to the motive that brought you hither. Although your worthy countenance was still well remembered by me, nevertheless, had I not with my own hand assisted to hang the Bashaw, you might, perhaps, have deceived even me. Now, however, I am here to propose a question."

"First of all, tell me why you came hither," interrupted Mustapha, full of resentment at finding himself detected.

"That I will explain to you," rejoined the other: "I could not put up with the Mighty any longer, and therefore ran away; but you, Mustapha, were properly the cause of our quarrel, and so you must give me your sister to wife, and I will help you in your flight; give her not, and I will go to my new master, and tell him something of our new Bashaw."

Mustapha was beside himself with fear and anger; at the very moment when he thought he had arrived at the happy accomplishment of his wishes, must this wretch come, and frustrate them all! It was the only way to carry his plan into execution—he must slay the little monster: with one bound, he sprang from the bed upon him; but the other, who might perhaps have anticipated something of the kind, let the lamp fall, which was immediately extinguished, and rushed forth in the dark, crying vehemently for help.

Now was the time for decisive action; the maids he was obliged, for the moment, to abandon, and attend only to his own safety: accordingly, he approached the window, to see if he could not spring from it. It was a tolerable distance from the ground, and on the other side stood a lofty wall, which he would have to surmount. Reflecting, he stood by the window until he heard many voices approaching his chamber: already were they at the door, when seizing desperately his dagger, and garments, he let himself down from the window. The fall was hard, but he felt that no bone was broken; immediately he sprang up, and ran to the wall which surrounded the court. This, to the astonishment of his pursuers, he mounted, and soon found himself at liberty. He ran on until he came to a little forest, where he sank down exhausted. Here he reflected on what was to be done; his horses and attendants he was obliged to leave behind, but the money, which he had placed in his girdle, he had saved.

His inventive genius, however, soon pointed him to another means of deliverance. He walked through the wood until he arrived at a village, where for a small sum he purchased a horse, with the help of which, in a short time, he reached a city. There he inquired for a physician, and was directed to an old experienced man. On this one he prevailed, by a few gold pieces, to furnish him with a medicine to produce a death-like sleep, which, by means of another, might be instantaneously removed. Having obtained this, he purchased a long false beard, a black gown, and various boxes and retorts, so that he could readily pass for a travelling physician; these articles he placed upon an ass, and rode back to the castle of Thiuli-Kos. He was certain, this time, of not being recognised, for the beard disfigured him so that he scarcely knew himself.

Arrived in the vicinity of the castle, he announced himself as the physician Chakamankabudibaba, and matters turned out as he had expected. The splendor of the name procured him extraordinary favor with the old fool, who invited him to table. Chakamankabudibaba appeared before Thiuli, and, having conversed with him scarcely an hour, the old man resolved that all his female slaves should submit to the examination of the wise physician. The latter could scarcely conceal his joy at the idea of once more beholding his beloved sister, and with palpitating heart followed Thiuli, who conducted him to his seraglio. They reached an unoccupied room, which was beautifully furnished.

"Chambaba, or whatever thou mayest be called, my good physician," said Thiuli-Kos, "look once at that hole in the wall; thence shall each of my slaves stretch forth her arm, and thou canst feel whether the pulse betoken sickness or health."

Answer as he might, Mustapha could not arrange it so that he might see them; nevertheless, Thiuli agreed to tell him, each time, the usual health of the one he was examining. Thiuli drew forth a long list from his girdle, and began, with loud voice, to call out, one by one, the names of his slaves; whereupon, each time, a hand came forth from the wall, and the physician felt the pulse. Six had been read off, and declared entirely well, when Thiuli, for the seventh called Fatima, and a small white hand slipped forth from the wall. Trembling with joy, Mustapha grasped it, and with an important air pronounced her seriously ill. Thiuli became very anxious, and commanded his wise Chakamankabudibaba straightway to prescribe some medicine for her. The physician left the room, and wrote a little scroll:

"Fatima, I will preserve thee, if thou canst make up thy mind to take a draught, which for two days will make thee dead; nevertheless, I possess the means of restoring thee to life. If thou wilt, then only return answer, that this liquid has been of no assistance, and it will be to me a token that thou agreest."

In a moment he returned to the room, where Thiuli had remained. He brought with him an innocent drink, felt the pulse of the sick Fatima once more, pushed the note beneath her bracelet, and then handed her the liquid through the opening in the wall. Thiuli seemed to be in great anxiety on Fatima's account, and postponed the examination of the rest to a more fitting opportunity. As he left the room with Mustapha, he addressed him in sorrowful accents:

"Chadibaba, tell me plainly, what thinkest thou of Fatima's illness?"

My brother answered with a deep sigh: "Ah, sir, may the Prophet give you consolation! she has a slow fever, which may, perhaps, cost her life!"

Then burned Thiuli's anger: "What sayest thou, cursed dog of a physician? She, for whom I gave two thousand gold pieces—shall she die like a cow? Know, if thou preservest her not, I will chop off thine head!"

My brother immediately saw that he had made a misstep, and again inspired Thiuli with hope. While they were yet conversing, a black slave came from the seraglio to tell the physician, that the drink had been of no assistance.

"Put forth all thy skill, Chakamdababelda, or whatever thy name may be; I will pay thee what thou askest!" cried out Thiuli-Kos, well-nigh howling with sorrow, at the idea of losing so much gold.

"I will give her a potion, which will put her out of all danger," answered the physician.

"Yes, yes!—give it her," sobbed the old Thiuli.

With joyful heart Mustapha went to bring his soporific, and having given it to the black slave, and shown him how much it was necessary to take for a dose, he went to Thiuli, and, telling him he must procure some medicinal herbs from the sea, hastened through the gate. On the shore, which was not far from the castle, he removed his false garments, and cast them into the water, where they floated merrily around; concealing himself, however, in a thicket, he awaited the night, and then stole softly to the burying-place of Thiuli's castle.

Hardly an hour had Mustapha been absent, when they brought Thiuli the intelligence that his slave Fatima was in the agonies of death. He sent them to the sea-coast to bring the physician back with all speed, but his messengers returned alone, with the news that the poor physician had fallen into the water, and was drowned; that they had espied his black gown floating upon the surface, and that now and then his large beard peeped forth from amid the billows. Thiuli seeing now no help, cursed himself and the whole world; plucked his beard, and dashed his head against the wall. But all this was of no use, for soon Fatima gave up the ghost, in the arms of her companions. When the unfortunate man heard the news of her death, he commanded them quickly to make a coffin, for he could not tolerate a dead person in his house; and bade them bear forth the corpse to the place of burial. The carriers brought in the coffin, but quickly set it down and fled, for they heard sighs and sobs among the other piles.

Mustapha, who, concealed behind the coffins, had inspired the attendants with such terror, came forth and lighted a lamp, which he had brought for that purpose. Then he drew out a vial which contained the life-restoring medicine, and lifted the lid of Fatima's coffin. But what amazement seized him, when by the light of the lamp, strange features met his gaze! Neither my sister, nor Zoraida, but an entire stranger, lay in the coffin! It was some time before he could recover from this new stroke of destiny; at last, however, compassion triumphed over anger. He opened the vial, and administered the liquid. She breathed—she opened her eyes—and seemed for some time to be reflecting where she was. At length, recalling all that had happened, she rose from the coffin, and threw herself, sobbing, at Mustapha's feet.

"How may I thank thee, excellent being," she exclaimed, "for having freed me from my frightful prison?" Mustapha interrupted her expressions of gratitude by inquiring, how it happened that she, and not his sister Fatima, had been preserved. The maiden looked in amazement.

"Now is my deliverance explained, which was before incomprehensible," answered she. "Know that in this castle I am called Fatima, and it was to me thou gavest thy note, and the preserving-drink."

My brother entreated her to give him intelligence of his sister and Zoraida, and learned that they were both in the castle, but, according to Thiuli's custom, had received different names; they were now called Mirza and Nurmahal. When Fatima, the rescued slave, saw that my brother was so cast down by this failure of his enterprise, she bade him take courage, and promised to show him means whereby he could still deliver both the maidens. Aroused by this thought, Mustapha was filled with new hope, and besought her to point out to him the way.

"Only five months," said she, "have I been Thiuli's slave; nevertheless, from the first, I have been continually meditating an escape; but for myself alone it was too difficult. In the inner court of the castle, you may have observed a fountain, which pours forth water from ten tubes; this fountain riveted my attention. I remembered in my father's house to have seen a similar one, the water of which was led up through a spacious aqueduct. In order to learn whether this fountain was constructed in the same manner, I one day praised its magnificence to Thiuli, and inquired after its architect. 'I myself built it,' answered he, 'and what thou seest here is still the smallest part; for the water comes hither into it from a brook at least a thousand paces off, flowing through a vaulted aqueduct, which is as high as a man. And all this have I myself planned.' After hearing this, I often wished only for a moment to have a man's strength, in order to roll away the stone from the side of the fountain; then could I have fled whither I would. The aqueduct now will I show to you; through it you can enter the castle by night, and set them free. Only you must have at least two men with you, in order to overpower the slaves which, by night, guard the seraglio."

Thus she spoke, and my brother Mustapha, although twice disappointed already in his expectations, once again took courage, and hoped with Allah's assistance to carry out the plan of the slave. He promised to conduct her in safety to her native land, if she would assist him in entering the castle. But one thought still troubled him, namely, where he could find two or three faithful assistants. Thereupon the dagger of Orbasan occurred to him, and the promise of the robber to hasten to his assistance, when he should stand in need of help, and he therefore started with Fatima from the burying-ground, to seek the chieftain.

In the same city where he had converted himself into a physician, with his last money he purchased a horse, and procured lodgings for Fatima, with a poor woman in the suburbs. He, however, hastened towards the mountain where he had first met Orbasan, and reached it in three days. He soon found the tent, and unexpectedly walked in before the chieftain, who welcomed him with friendly courtesy. He related to him his unsuccessful attempts, whereupon the grave Orbasan could not restrain himself from laughing a little now and then, particularly when he announced himself as the physician Chakamankabudibaba. At the treachery of the little man, however, he was furious; and swore, if he could find him, to hang him with his own hand. He assured my brother that he was ready to assist him the moment he should be sufficiently recovered from his ride. Accordingly, Mustapha remained that night again in the robber's tent, and with the first morning-red they set out, Orbasan taking with him three of his bravest men, well mounted and armed. They rode rapidly, and in two days arrived at the little city, where Mustapha had left the rescued Fatima. Thence they rode on with her unto the forest, from which, at a little distance, they could see Thiuli's castle; there they concealed themselves, to await the night. As soon as it was dark, guided by Fatima, they proceeded softly to the brook, where the aqueduct commenced, and soon found it. There they left Fatima and a servant with the horses, and prepared themselves for the descent: before they started, however, Fatima once more repeated, with precision, the directions she had given; namely, that, on emerging from the fountain into the inner court-yard, they would find a tower in each corner on the right and left; that inside the sixth gate from the right tower, they would find Fatima and Zoraida, guarded by two black slaves. Well provided with weapons and iron implements for forcing the doors, Mustapha, Orbasan, and the two other men, descended through the aqueduct; they sank, indeed, in water, up to the middle, but not the less vigorously on that account did they press forward.

In a half hour they arrived at the fountain, and immediately began to ply their tools. The wall was thick and firm, but could not long resist the united strength of the four men; they soon made a breach sufficiently large to allow them to slip through without difficulty. Orbasan was the first to emerge, and then assisted the others. Being now all in the court-yard, they examined the side of the castle which lay before them, in order to find the door which had been described. But they could not agree as to which it was, for on counting from the right tower to the left, they found one door which had been walled up, and they knew not whether Fatima had included this in her calculation. But Orbasan was not long in making up his mind: "My good sword will open to me this gate," he exclaimed, advancing to the sixth, while the others followed him. They opened it, and found six black slaves lying asleep upon the floor; imagining that they had missed the object of their search, they were already softly drawing back, when a figure raised itself in the corner, and in well-known accents called for help. It was the little man of the robber-encampment. But ere the slaves knew what had taken place, Orbasan sprang upon the little man, tore his girdle in two, stopped his mouth, and bound his hands behind his back; then he turned to the slaves, some of whom were already half bound by Mustapha and the two others, and assisted in completely overpowering them. They presented their daggers to the breasts of the slaves, and asked where Nurmahal and Mirza were: they confessed that they were in the next chamber. Mustapha rushed into the room, and found Fatima and Zoraida awakened by the noise. They were not long in collecting their jewels and garments, and following my brother.

Meanwhile the two robbers proposed to Orbasan to carry off what they could find, but he forbade them, saying: "It shall never be told of Orbasan, that he enters houses by night, to steal gold." Mustapha, and those he had preserved, quickly stepped into the aqueduct, whither Orbasan promised to follow them immediately. As soon as they had departed, the chieftain and one of the robbers led forth the little man into the court-yard; there, having fastened around his neck a silken cord, which they had brought for that purpose, they hung him on the highest point of the fountain. After having thus punished the treachery of the wretch, they also entered the aqueduct, and followed Mustapha. With tears the two maidens thanked their brave preserver, Orbasan; but he urged them in haste to their flight, for it was very probable that Thiuli-Kos would seek them in every direction.

With deep emotion, on the next day, did Mustapha and the rescued maidens part with Orbasan. Indeed, they never will forget him! Fatima, the freed slave, left us in disguise for Balsora, in order to take passage thence to her native land.

After a short and agreeable journey, my brother and his companions reached home. Delight at seeing them once more, almost killed my old father; the next day after their arrival, he gave a great festival, to which all the city was invited. Before a large assemblage of relations and friends, my brother had to relate his story, and with one voice they praised him and the noble robber.

When, however, Mustapha had finished, my father arose and led Zoraida to him. "Thus remove I," said he with solemn voice, "the curse from thy head; take this maiden as the reward which thy unwearied courage has merited. Receive my fatherly blessing: and may there never be wanting to our city, men who, in brotherly love, in prudence, and bravery, may be thy equals!"

The Caravan had reached the end of the desert, and gladly did the travellers salute the green meadows, and thickly-leaved trees, of whose charms they had been deprived for so many days. In a lovely valley lay a caravansery, which they selected as their resting-place for the night; and though it offered but limited accommodations and refreshment, still was the whole company more happy and sociable than ever: for the thought of having passed through the dangers and hardships, with which a journey through the desert is ever accompanied, had opened every heart, and attuned their minds to jest and gayety. Muley, the young and merry merchant, went through a comic dance, and sang songs thereto, which elicited a laugh, even from Zaleukos, the serious Greek. But not content with having raised the spirits of his comrades by dance and merriment, he also gave them, in the best style, the story he had promised, and, as soon as he could recover breath from his gambols, began the following tale.

LITTLE MUCK

IN Nicea, my beloved father-city, lived a man, whom people called "Little Muck." Though at that time I was quite young, I can recollect him very well, particularly since, on one occasion, I was flogged almost to death, by my father, on his account. The Little Muck, even then, when I knew him, an old man, was nevertheless but three or four feet high: he had a singular figure, for his body, little and smart as it was, carried a head much larger and thicker than that of others. He lived all alone in a large house, and even cooked for himself; moreover, it would not have been known in the city whether he was alive or dead, (for he went forth but once in four weeks,) had not every day, about the hour of noon, strong fumes come forth from the house. Nevertheless, in the evening he was often to be seen walking to and fro upon his roof; although, from the street, it seemed as if it were his head alone that was running around there.

I and my comrades were wicked fellows, who teased and ridiculed every one; accordingly, to us it was a holiday when the Little Muck went forth: on the appointed day we would assemble before his house, and wait for him to come out. When, then, the door opened, and at first the immense head and still larger turban peered forth, when the rest of the body followed covered with a small cloak which had been irregularly curtailed, with wide pantaloons, and a broad girdle in which hung a long dagger, so long that one could not tell whether Muck was fastened to the dagger, or the dagger to Muck—when in this guise he came forth, then would the air resound with our cries of joy; then would we fling our caps aloft, and dance round him, like mad. Little Muck, however, would salute us with a serious bow, and walk with long strides through the street, shuffling now and then his feet, for he wore large wide slippers, such as I have never elsewhere seen. We boys would run behind him, crying continually, "Little Muck! Little Muck!" We also had a droll little verse, which we would now and then sing in his honor; it ran thus:—

"Little Muck, oh Little Muck! What a fine, brave dwarf art thou! Livest in a house so tall; Goest forth but once a month, Mountain-headed, though so small. Turn thyself but once, and look! Run, and catch us, Little Muck."

In this way had we often carried on our sport, and, to my shame, I must confess that I took the most wicked part in it, for I often plucked him by the mantle, and once trod from behind on his large slippers, so that he fell down. This was, at first, a source of the greatest amusement to me, but my laughter soon ceased when I saw the Little Muck go up to my father's house; he walked straight in, and remained there some time. I concealed myself near the door, and saw Muck come forth again, escorted by my father, who respectfully shook his hand, and with many bows parted with him at the door. My mind was uneasy, and I remained some time in my concealment; at length, however, hunger, which I feared more than blows, drove me in, and ashamed and with downcast head, I walked in before my father.

"Thou hast, as I hear, insulted the good Muck," said he with a very serious tone. "I will tell thee the history of this Muck, and then I am sure thou wilt ridicule him no more. But first, thou shalt receive thy allowance." The allowance was five-and-twenty lashes, which he took care to count only too honestly. He thereupon took a long pipe-stem, unscrewed the amber mouthpiece, and beat me more severely than he had ever done before.

When the five-and-twenty were all made up, he commanded me to attend, and told me the following story of Little Muck.

The father of Little Muck, who is properly called Mukrah, lived here in Nicea, a respectable, but poor man. He kept himself almost as retired as his son does now. The latter he could not endure, because he was ashamed of his dwarfish figure, and let him therefore grow up in perfect ignorance. When the Little Muck was still in his seventeenth year, a merry child, his father, a grave man, kept continually reproaching him, that he, who ought long before to have trodden down the shoes of infancy, was still so stupid and childish.

The old man, however, one day had a bad fall, from the effects of which he died, and Little Muck was left behind, poor and ignorant. His cruel relations, to whom the deceased owed more than he could pay, turned the poor fellow out of the house, and advised him to go forth into the world, and seek his fortune. Muck answered that he was all ready, only asking them for his father's dress, which they willingly granted him. His father had been a large, portly man, and the garments on that account did not fit him. Muck, however, soon hit upon an expedient; he cut off what was too long, and then put them on. He seemed, however, to have forgotten that he must also take from their width; hence the strange dress that he wears at the present day; the huge turban, the broad girdle, the wide breeches, the blue cloak, all these he has inherited from his father, and worn ever since. The long Damascus dagger of his father, too, he attached to his girdle, and seizing a little staff, set out from the door.

Gayly he wandered, the whole day, for he had set out to seek his fortune: if he saw upon the ground a potsherd shining in the sunlight, he took care to pick it up, in the belief that he could change it into a diamond of the first water; if he saw in the distance the cupola of a Mosque sparkling like fire, or the sea glittering like a mirror, he would hasten up, fully persuaded that he had arrived at fairy-land. But ah! these phantoms vanished as he approached, and too soon fatigue, and his stomach gnawed by hunger, convinced him that he was still in the land of mortals. In this way he travelled two days, in hunger and grief, and despaired of finding his fortune; the produce of the field was his only support, the hard earth his bed. On the morning of the third day, he espied a large city upon an eminence. Brightly shone the crescent upon her pinnacles, variegated flags waved over the roofs, and seemed to be beckoning Little Muck to themselves. In surprise he stood still, contemplating the city and the surrounding country.

"There at length will Klein-Muck find his fortune," said he to himself, and in spite of his fatigue bounded in the air; "there or nowhere!" He collected all his strength, and walked towards the city. But although the latter seemed quite near, he could not reach it until mid-day, for his little limbs almost entirely refused him their assistance, and he was obliged to sit down to rest in the shade of a palm-tree. At last he reached the gate; he fixed the mantle jauntily, wound the turban still more tastily around his head, made the girdle broader, and arranged the dagger so as to fall still more obliquely: then, wiping the dust from his shoes, and seizing his cane, he marched bravely through the gate.

He had already wandered through a few streets, but nowhere did any door open to him, nowhere did any one exclaim, as he had anticipated: "Little Muck, come in and eat and drink, and rest thy little feet."

He was looking very wistfully straight at a large fine house, when a window opened, and an old woman, putting out her head, exclaimed in a singing tone—

"Hither, come hither! The porridge is here; The table I've spread, Come taste of my cheer. Hither, come hither! The porridge is hot; Your neighbors bring with you, To dip in the pot!"

The door opened, and Muck saw many dogs and cats walking in. For a moment he stood in doubt whether he should accept the invitation; at last, however, he took heart and entered the mansion.

Before him proceeded a couple of genteel kittens, and he resolved to follow them, since they, perhaps, knew the way to the kitchen better than himself.

When Muck had ascended the steps, he met the same old woman who had looked forth from the window. With frowning air she asked what he wanted.

"Thou hast invited every one to thy porridge," answered Little Muck, "and as I was very hungry, I came too."

The old woman laughed, saying, "Whence come you then, strange fellow? The whole city knows that I cook for no one but my dear cats, and now and then, as you see, I invite their companions from the neighborhood." Little Muck told her how hard it had gone with him since his father's death, and entreated her to let him dine, that day, with her cats. The old woman, on whom the frank relation of the little fellow made quite an impression, permitted him to become her guest, and gave him abundance to eat and drink. When he was satisfied and refreshed, she looked at him for some time, and then said:—

"Little Muck, remain with me in my service; you will have little to do, and shall be well taken care of." Muck, who had relished the cat-porridge, agreed, and thus became the servant of the Frau Ahavzi. His duties were light but singular: Frau Ahavzi had two male, and four female cats; every morning Little Muck had to comb their hair, and anoint them with costly ointment. When the Frau went out, he had to give them all his attention; when they ate, he placed their bowls before them; and, at night, he had to lay them on silken cushions, and wrap them up in velvet coverings. There were, moreover, a few little dogs in the house, on which he was obliged to wait; but there were not so many ceremonies gone through with these as with the cats, whom Frau Ahavzi treated as her own children. As for the rest, Muck led as retired a life as in his father's house, for with the exception of the Frau, he saw every day only dogs and cats.

For a long time it went very well with Little Muck; he had enough to eat, and but little to do; and the old woman seemed to be perfectly satisfied with him. But, by-and-by, the cats began to behave very badly; the moment the Frau went out, they ran around the rooms as if possessed, threw down every thing in confusion, and broke considerable fine crockery, which stood in their way. When, however, they heard their mistress coming up the steps, they would creep to their cushions, and wag their tails, when they saw her, as if nothing had happened. The Frau Ahavzi always fell in a passion when she saw her rooms so disordered, and attributed all to Muck; assert his innocence as he might, she believed her cats who looked so demure, in preference to her servant.

Little Muck was very sorry that here also he had been disappointed in finding his fortune, and determined in his own mind to leave the service of the Frau Ahavzi. As, however, on his first journey, he had learned how badly one lives without money, he resolved to procure, in some way, for himself the wages which his mistress had once promised him, but had never paid. In the house of the Frau Ahavzi was a room, which was always closed, and the inside of which he had never seen. Nevertheless, he had often heard the Frau making a noise therein, and he would have willingly risked his life to know what was there concealed. Reflecting upon his travelling-money, it occurred to him that there his mistress might conceal her treasures. But the door was always tightly closed, and therefore he could not get at them.

One morning, after the Frau Ahavzi had gone out, one of the little dogs who was treated by her in a very stepmother-like manner, but whose favor he had in a great degree gained by various acts of kindness, pulled him by his wide pantaloons, and acted as if he wanted Muck to follow him. Muck, who always gladly played with him, did so, and perceived that the dog was leading him to the sleeping apartment of his mistress; he stopped before a door, which the little fellow had never before observed, and which was now wide open. The dog entered, and Muck, following, was overjoyed at finding himself in the very chamber, which had so long been the object of his curiosity. He looked all around for money, but could find none: old garments only, and strangely-fashioned vases were scattered around. One of the latter, in particular, attracted his attention; it was of crystal, and fine figures were cut thereon. He lifted it up and turned it on all sides; but, oh horror! he had not observed that it had a lid, which was but insecurely fastened on: it fell to the floor, and broke into a thousand pieces.

For a long time stood Little Muck motionless through terror; now was his fate decided, now must he fly, or be killed by the old woman. His departure was immediately resolved on; he only looked around, to see if he could not use some of the goods of the Frau Ahavzi upon his journey. Thereupon, a formidable pair of huge slippers met his eye; they were not, it is true, beautiful, but his own could hold out no longer; moreover their size was an inducement, for when he had these upon his feet, people would see, he hoped, that he had cast off the shoes of childhood. He quickly took off his own slippers, and put on the others. A walking-stick, also, with a fine lion's head cut upon the handle, seemed to be standing too idly in the corner; so he seized it, and hurried from the apartment. He hastened to his own room, put on his cloak, arranged his paternal turban, placed the dagger in his girdle, and ran as fast as his feet would carry him, out of the house, and out of the city. Fear of his old mistress drove him farther and still farther, until, from fatigue, he could scarcely run any more. He had never gone so quickly in his life; nay, it appeared to him as if he could not cease running, for an invisible power seemed propelling him on. At last he observed that this must be connected with the slippers, for they would continually shoot forward and bear him along with them. He endeavored in various ways, to stand still, but could not succeed; at last, in the greatest distress, he cried out to himself, as a man calls to his horse, "Wo—wo!" Then the slippers stopped, and Muck fell exhausted upon the earth.

The slippers were a source of great joy to him. Thus had he, by his services, gained something that would help him on his way through the world to seek his fortune. In spite of his joy, he fell asleep through fatigue; for the body of Little Muck, which had to carry so heavy a head, could not hold out long. In his dream the little dog appeared to him, which had assisted him to the slippers in the house of the Frau Ahavzi, and thus spoke:—

"Dear Muck, thou dost not still rightly understand the use of the slippers: know that if, in them, thou turnest thyself three times around upon the heel, thou canst fly wherever thou wilt; and with the staff thou canst find treasures, for, wherever gold is buried, it will beat three times upon the earth; where silver, twice."

Thus dreamed Little Muck. When he awoke, he reflected on the singular vision, and resolved to make the experiment immediately. He put on the slippers, lifted one foot, and began to turn around upon his heel. But whoever has attempted to perform this manœuvre in an enormously wide slipper, will not wonder that the Little Muck could not succeed, particularly when he remembers that his heavy head kept falling on this side and on that.

The poor little fellow fell several times violently upon his nose; nevertheless, that did not deter him from making the trial again, and at last he succeeded. Like a wheel he went around upon his heel, wishing himself in the nearest large city, and—the slippers mounted into the air, ran with the speed of the wind through the clouds, and before Little Muck knew what to make of it, he found himself in a large market-place, where many stalls were erected, and innumerable men were busily running to and fro. He moved among the people, but considered it more prudent to retire into a less frequented street, for near the market one of the slippers bore him along so rapidly, that he almost fell down, or else ran against one and another with his projecting dagger, so that it was with difficulty he avoided their blows.

Little Muck now seriously reflected what he should set about, in order to earn a piece of money. He had, it is true, a staff which would show him concealed treasures, but how could he find a place where gold or silver was buried. He could, indeed, in this emergency, have exhibited himself for money, but for this he was too proud. At last the quickness of his gait occurred to him. Perhaps, thought he, my slippers can procure me support, and he determined to hire himself out as a courier. He ventured to hope that the king of the city rewarded such service well, so he inquired for the palace. Before the door of the palace stood a guard, who asked him what he sought there. On answering that he was in search of service, they led him to the overseer of the slaves. Before this one he laid his request, and entreated that he might be admitted among the royal couriers. The overseer measured him with his eyes from head to foot, and said: "How! with thy little feet, which are scarcely a span long, wishest thou to become a royal messenger? Away with thee! I cannot play with every fool."

Little Muck assured him, however, that his proposal was made in perfect seriousness, and that he would let it come to a trial with the swiftest, upon a wager. The matter seemed very ludicrous to the overseer. He commanded him to hold himself in readiness for a race in the afternoon, and leading him into the kitchen, saw that he was furnished with proper meat and drink. He himself, however, repaired unto the king, and told him of the little man and his proposal. The king was a merry lord, and therefore it pleased him well that the overseer had kept the little man for their amusement. He directed him to make preparations in a large meadow behind the castle, that the race might be conveniently beheld by his whole court, and once more commanded him to take great care of the dwarf. The king told his princes, and princesses, what a pastime they were to enjoy that afternoon; these told it again to their attendants, and when the time arrived all were in great expectation; and as many as had feet poured into the meadow, where a scaffolding had been erected, in order to see the boastful dwarf run.

As soon as the king and his sons and daughters had taken their places upon the platform, the Little Muck walked forth upon the meadow, and made before the noble sovereign a very elegant bow. A universal cry of joy arose, the moment they beheld the little fellow; such a figure had they never seen. The small body with the mighty head, the little cloak, and the wide pantaloons, the long dagger in the broad girdle, the tiny feet in the immense slippers—no! it was so droll a sight they could not keep from laughing aloud. Little Muck, however, was not disconcerted by their laughter. He proudly walked forward, supported by his cane, and awaited his opponent. At Muck's own desire, the overseer of the slaves had selected the best runner. Walking in, he placed himself near the dwarf, and both looked for the signal. Thereupon the Princess Amarza made a sign with her veil as had been preconcerted, and, like two arrows shot from the same bow, the racers flew over the meadow.

At first the courier took a tremendous bound, but Muck pursued him in his slipper carriage, overtook him, passed him, and had been standing for some time at the goal, when his opponent, gasping for breath, ran up. Amazement for a few moments enchained the spectators: the king was the first to clap his hands; then shouted the crowd for joy, all exclaiming, "Long live the Little Muck, the victor in the race!"

Meanwhile they had brought up the little man; he prostrated himself before the king, saying, "Most mighty King, I have here given thee but a small proof of my powers; allow them, I pray thee, to give me a place among thy couriers." The king answered:—

"Nay, dear Muck, thou shalt be my favorite messenger, and shalt remain about my person; every year shalt thou have a hundred gold pieces as thy wages, and thou shalt sup at the table of my first attendant."

Then Muck thought he had at last found the fortune, of which he had so long been in search, and was merry and light-hearted. Moreover, he rejoiced in the peculiar favor of the king, for the latter employed him on his quickest and most secret errands, which he performed with the greatest care, and with inconceivable rapidity.

But the other attendants of the king were not well affected towards him, because they reluctantly saw themselves displaced from their lord's favor by a dwarf, who knew how to do nothing, but to run fast. They set on foot many a conspiracy against him in order to work his destruction, but all failed, through the confidence which the king placed in his private Oberleibläufer, (for to this dignity had he in so short a time arrived.)

Muck, upon whom these movements against himself produced no effect, thought not of revenge; for that he had too good a heart: no, he reflected upon the means of making himself necessary to his enemies, and beloved by them. Thereupon the staff, which in his good fortune he had forgotten, occurred to him; if he could find treasures, he thought the lords would be more favorably disposed towards him. He had before this often heard that the father of the present king had buried much of his gold, when the enemy had invaded the land; they said, moreover, that he had died without imparting the secret to his son. From this time Muck always carried his cane, in the hope that he would some time pass over the place where the money of the old king was buried.

One evening, chance led him into a remote portion of the castle-garden, which he seldom visited, when suddenly he felt the staff move in his hand, and three times it beat upon the ground. He knew in an instant what this indicated; accordingly he drew forth his dagger, made marks on the surrounding trees, and then slipped back into the castle. Then he procured a spade, and awaited night for his undertaking.

Treasure-digging, however, gave Muck more trouble than he had anticipated. His arms were very feeble, his spade large and heavy; he might perhaps have been laboring a couple of hours, without getting any farther down than as many feet. At length he hit upon something hard, which sounded like iron: he then set to work still more diligently, and soon brought up a large cover; he then descended into the hole, in order to examine what the cover concealed, and found a large pot completely full of gold pieces. His feeble wisdom, however, did not teach him to lift up the pot; but he put in his pantaloons and girdle as much as he could carry, filled his cloak, and then carefully covering up the rest, placed the load upon his back. But, indeed, if he had not had the slippers on his feet, he could not have stirred, so heavily did the gold weigh him down. Then, unobserved, he reached his room, and secured the money under the cushions of his sofa.

When the little man saw so much gold in his possession, he thought the tables would now be turned, and that from among his enemies at court, he could gain many well-wishers and warm friends. But even in this, one could see that the good Muck had enjoyed no very careful education; otherwise he would not have imagined that he could buy true friends with gold. Ah! that he had then put on his slippers, and with his mantle full of gold, scampered away!

The gold which from this time Little Muck distributed with lavish hand, awakened the envy of the other court-attendants. The kitchen-master, Ahuli, said, "He is a counterfeiter." The slave-overseer, Achmet, said, "He has cajoled the king." But Archaz, the treasurer, his most wicked enemy, who himself, even, now and then put his hand into his lord's coffers, exclaimed, "He is a thief." In order to be sure of the thing, they consulted together, and the head cup-bearer, Korchuz, placed himself one day, with a very sorrowful and depressed air, before the eyes of the king. He made his wo so apparent, that the king asked him what was the matter.

"Ah!" answered he, "I am sorry that I have lost the favor of my lord!"

"Why talkest thou idly, friend Korchuz?" rejoined the monarch. "Since when have I veiled from thee the sun of my favor?"

The cup-bearer answered, that he loaded his private Oberleibläufer with money, but gave his poor faithful servants nothing. The king was much astonished at this accusation, had the story of Muck's gold-distribution told him, and the conspirators soon aroused in him the suspicion that the dwarf had, in some way or other, stolen the money from the treasure-chamber. Very pleasant was this turn of the matter to the treasurer, who would not otherwise have willingly submitted his accounts to examination. The king thereupon commanded that they should secretly watch all the movements of the dwarf, in order, if possible, to surprise him in the act. When, now, on the night which followed the fatal day, seeing his funds almost exhausted by his generosity, Muck crept forth, with his spade, into the castle-garden, to bring new supplies from his secret treasury, the watch followed him in the distance, led by Ahuli and Archaz; and, at the moment when he was removing the gold from the pot to his cloak, they fell upon him, bound him, and immediately led him before the king. The latter, whom, independently of any thing else, this interruption of his sleep would have enraged, received his poor dwarf very ungraciously, and ordered an immediate trial. Meanwhile they had dug the full pot out of the ground, and with the spade and cloak full of gold had placed it before the king. The treasurer said that he had surprised Muck with his guard, just as he had buried this vessel of gold in the earth.

The king thereupon inquired of the accused, whether it was true, and whence the gold had come.

Little Muck, conscious of innocence, answered that he had discovered this pot in the garden; that he had not buried it, but had brought it to light.

All present laughed aloud at this defence; the king, however, provoked in the highest degree by the supposed impudence of the dwarf, exclaimed, "How, wretch! wilt thou so stupidly and shamelessly lie to thy king, after having stolen from him? Treasurer Archaz, I command thee to say whether thou knowest this sum of gold to be the same that is missing from my treasury."

The treasurer thereupon answered that he was sure of the thing; that so much and even more had been missing from the royal treasures; and he could take his oath that this was the stolen money. Then the king commanded them to place Little Muck in galling chains, and convey him to prison: to Archaz, however, he gave the gold, that he might restore it to the treasury. Delighted at the fortunate issue of the matter, the officer took it, and counted out, at home, the glittering gold pieces; but the bad man never disclosed that down in the pot lay a letter, to the following purport:—

"The enemy has overrun my land; therefore I here conceal a portion of my treasure. Whoever may find it, the curse of his king fall upon him, if he do not immediately deliver it to my son!

King Sadi."

In his dungeon, poor Muck gave way to sorrowful reflections; he knew that for taking royal property death was the penalty; and yet—he could not betray the secret of his staff unto the king, because, in that case, he justly feared being deprived of both that, and his slippers. His slippers, alas! could render him no help, for there by close fetters he was fastened to the wall, and, torment himself as he might, he could not turn around upon his heel. When, however, on the next day, sentence of death was pronounced, he thought it would be better to live without the magic staff, than to die with it; and, having asked a private audience with the king, disclosed to him the secret. At first the king gave no credit to his assertions, but Little Muck promised him a proof, if he would respite him from death. The king gave him his word upon it, and having had some gold buried in the earth, unseen by Muck, commanded him to find it with his cane. In a few moments he succeeded in doing so, for the staff beat three times distinctly upon the ground. Then the king saw that his treasurer had betrayed him, and sent him, as is customary in the East, a silken cord, wherewith he should strangle himself. To Little Muck, however, he said:—

"I have indeed promised thee thy life, but it seems to me that this is not the only secret thou art possessed of, connected with this staff. Therefore thou shalt remain in everlasting captivity, if thou do not confess what relation exists between it and thy rapid running."

Little Muck, whom one night in his dungeon had deprived of all desire for further confinement, acknowledged that his whole art lay in the slippers; nevertheless, he informed not the king of the wonderful effect of turning three times upon the heel. The king put on the slippers, himself, in order to make the experiment, and ran, like mad, through the garden; often did he wish to hold up, but he knew not how to bring the slippers to a halt, and Muck, who could not deny himself this revenge, let him run on, until he fell down exhausted.

When the king returned to consciousness, he was terribly angry at Little Muck, who had suffered him to run until so entirely out of breath. "I have promised thee thy freedom and life," said he, "but within twelve hours must thou leave my land; otherwise will I have thee hung." The slippers and cane, however, he commanded them to bear to his treasure-chamber.

Thus, poor as ever, wandered the little fellow forth through the land, cursing the folly which had led him astray, and prevented his playing an important part at court. The land from which he was banished, was fortunately not extensive, and accordingly eight hours brought him to the frontier; but travelling, now that he was used to his dear slippers, came very hard to him. Having arrived at the border, he chose the usual road for reaching the most lonely part of the forest, for he hated all men, and resolved to live there by himself. In a thick portion of the wood, he lighted on a place, which seemed to him quite suitable for the resolution he had taken. A clear brook, surrounded by large shady fig-trees, and a soft turf, invited him: he threw himself down, determined to taste food no more, but calmly to await his end. Amid his sorrowful reflections on death, he fell asleep; when he awoke, he was tormented by hunger, and began to think that starving to death was rather an unpleasant affair; so he looked around to find something to eat.

Fine ripe figs hung upon the tree beneath which he had slept; he stretched forth his hand to pluck some; their taste was delicious, and then he descended into the brook to slake his thirst. But what was his horror, when the water showed his head adorned with two immense ears, and a long thick nose! Amazed, he clapped his hands upon his ears, and they were really more than half an ell long.

"I deserve ass's ears!" he exclaimed; "for, like an ass, have I trodden Fortune under my feet." He wandered around among the trees, and feeling hunger again, was obliged to have recourse once more to the fig-tree, for he could find nothing else that was eatable. After the second portion of figs, it struck him that if his ears could find room beneath his large turban, he would not look so ridiculous, and, on trying it, he found that his ears had vanished. He ran straight back to the stream, in order to convince himself thereof; it was actually so; his ears had resumed their original figure, his long misshapen nose was no more! He soon perceived how all this had happened; from the first fig-tree he had received the long nose and ears, the second had relieved him of them: he saw with joy that kind destiny yet again placed in his hands the means of becoming fortunate. He plucked, therefore, from each tree as many figs as he could carry, and went back to the land which shortly before he had left. There, in the first town, he disguised himself by means of different garments; then, turning again to the city inhabited by the king, he soon arrived at it.

For about a year ripe fruit had been quite scarce; Little Muck, therefore, placed himself before the gate of the palace, for from his former residence there, it was well known to him, that here such rareties would be purchased by the kitchen-master for the royal table. Muck had not long been seated, when he saw that dignitary walking across the court-yard. He examined the articles of the traders who had placed themselves at the palace-gate; at length his eye fell upon Muck's little basket.

"Ah! a dainty morsel!" said he, "which will certainly please his majesty: what wish you for the whole basket?" Muck set a high price upon them, and the bargain was soon struck. The kitchen-master gave the basket to his slave, and went his way: meantime Little Muck stole away, for he feared, when the change should show itself on the heads of the court, that he, as the one who sold them, would be sought for punishment.

At table the king was well pleased, and praised his kitchen-master more than ever, on account of his good kitchen, and the care with which he always sought the rarest morsels for his table; the officer, however, who well knew what dainties he had in the back-ground, smiled pleasantly, and let fall but few words: "The day is not all past till evening," or "End good, all good;" so that the princesses were very curious to know what he would still bring on. The moment, however, he had the fine, inviting figs set upon the table, a universal "Ah!" escaped the lips of those who were present. "How ripe! how delicate!" exclaimed the king; "kitchen-master, thou art a whole-souled man, and deservest our peculiar favor!" Thus speaking, the king, who with such choice dishes took care to be very sparing, with his own hands distributed the figs around the table. Each prince and princess received two; the ladies of the court, the Viziers and Agas, each one; the rest he placed before himself, and began to swallow them with great delight.

"In the name of heaven, father, why lookest thou so strange?" suddenly exclaimed the Princess Amarza. All gazed in astonishment upon the king; vast ears hung down from his head, a long nose stretched itself bridge-like, over above his chin; upon themselves also they looked, one upon another, with amazement and horror; all, more or less, were adorned with the same strange headdress.

The horror of the court may be imagined. All the physicians in the city were immediately sent for; they came with a blustering air, prescribed pills and mixtures, but ears and noses remained. They operated on one of the princes, but the ears grew out again.

From the place of concealment into which he had withdrawn, Muck had heard the whole story, and perceived that it was now time for him to commence operations. He had already, with the money obtained by the sale of his figs, procured a dress which would represent him as a learned man; a long beard of goat's hair completed the illusion. With a small sack full of figs he repaired to the royal palace, and offered his assistance as a foreign physician. At first they were quite incredulous; but when Little Muck gave a fig to one of the princes, and thereby restored ears and nose to their original shape, then were all eager to be cured by the stranger. But the king took him silently by the hand, and led him to his apartment; then, opening a door that led into the treasure-chamber, he made signs to Muck to follow.

"Here are my treasures," said the king; "choose for thyself: whatever it may be, it shall be thine, if thou wilt free me from this shameful evil." This was sweet music in the ears of Little Muck: at the moment of entering he had seen his slippers standing upon the floor, and hard by lay his little staff. He moved around the room, as if in wonder at the royal treasures; but no sooner had he reached his beloved shoes, than he hastily slipped into them, and seizing the little cane, tore off his false beard, and displayed to the astonished king the well-known countenance of his exiled Muck.

"False king!" said he, "who rewardest faithful service with ingratitude, take, as well-deserved punishment, the deformity which thou now hast. The ears I leave thee, that, each day they may remind thee of Little Muck." Having thus spoken, he turned quickly around upon his heel, wished himself far away, and before the king could call for help Little Muck had vanished. Ever since, he has lived here in great affluence, but alone, for men he despises. Experience has made him a wise man—one who, though there is something offensive in his exterior, deserves rather your admiration than your ridicule.

Such was my father's story. I assured him that I sincerely repented of my behavior towards the good little man, and he remitted the other half of the punishment which he had intended for me. To my comrades I told the wonderful history of the dwarf, and we conceived such an affection for him, that no one insulted him any more. On the contrary, we honored him as long as he lived, and bowed as low to him as to Cadi or Mufti.

The travellers determined to rest a day in this caravansery, in order to refresh themselves and their beasts for the rest of their journey. The gayety of the day before again prevailed, and they diverted themselves with various sports. After the meal, however, they called upon the fifth merchant, Ali Sizah, to perform his duty to the rest, and give them a story. He answered, that his life was too poor in remarkable adventures for him to relate one connected therewith, but he would tell them something which had no relation to it: "The story of the False Prince."

THE FALSE PRINCE.

THE FALSE PRINCE

THERE was once an honest journeyman tailor, by name Labakan, who learned his trade with an excellent master in Alexandria. It could not be said that Labakan was unhandy with the needle; on the contrary, he could make excellent work: moreover, one would have done him injustice to have called him lazy. Nevertheless, his companions knew not what to make of him, for he would often sew for hours together so rapidly that the needle would glow in his hand, and the thread smoke, and that none could equal him. At another time, however, (and this, alas! happened more frequently,) he would sit in deep meditation, looking with his staring eyes straight before him, and with a countenance and air so peculiar, that his master and fellow-journeymen could say of his appearance nothing else than, "Labakan has on again, his aristocratic face."

On Friday, however, when others quietly returned home from prayers to their labor, Labakan would come forth from the mosque in a fine garment which with great pains he had made for himself, and walk with slow and haughty steps through the squares and streets of the city. At such times, if one of his companions cried, "Joy be with thee!" or, "How goes it, friend Labakan?" he would patronizingly give a token of recognition with his hand, or, if he felt called upon to be very polite, would bow genteelly with the head. Whenever his master said to him in jest, "Labakan, in thee a prince is lost," he would be rejoiced, and answer, "Have you too observed it?" or, "I have already long thought it."

In this manner did the honest journeyman tailor conduct himself for a long time, while his master tolerated his folly, because, in other respects, he was a good man and an excellent workman. But one day, Selim, the sultan's brother, who was travelling through Alexandria, sent a festival-garment to his master to have some change made in it, and the master gave it to Labakan, because he did the finest work. In the evening, when the apprentices had all gone forth to refresh themselves after the labor of the day, an irresistible desire drove Labakan back into the workshop, where the garment of the sultan's brother was hanging. He stood some time, in reflection, before it, admiring now the splendor of the embroidery, now the varied colors of the velvet and silk. He cannot help it, he must put it on; and, lo! it fits him as handsomely as if it were made for him. "Am not I as good a prince as any?" asked he of himself, as he strutted up and down the room. "Has not my master himself said, that I was born for a prince?" With the garments, the apprentice seemed to have assumed quite a kingly carriage; he could believe nothing else, than that he was a king's son in obscurity, and as such he resolved to travel forth into the world, leaving a city where the people hitherto had been so foolish as not to discover his innate dignity beneath the veil of his inferior station. The splendid garment seemed sent to him by a good fairy; resolving therefore not to slight so precious a gift, he put his little stock of money in his pocket, and, favored by the darkness of the night, wandered forth from Alexandria's gates.

The new prince excited admiration everywhere upon his route, for the splendid garment, and his serious majestic air, would not allow him to pass for a common pedestrian. If one inquired of him about it, he took care to answer, with a mysterious look, that he had his reasons for it. Perceiving, however, that he rendered himself an object of ridicule by travelling on foot, he purchased for a small sum an old horse, which suited him very well, for it never brought his habitual quiet and mildness into difficulty, by compelling him to show himself off as an excellent rider, a thing which in reality he was not.

One day, as he was proceeding on his way, step by step, upon his Murva, (thus had he named his horse,) a stranger joined him, and asked permission to travel in his company, since to him the distance would seem much shorter, in conversation with another. The rider was a gay young man, elegant and genteel in manners. He soon knit up a conversation with Labakan, with respect to his whence and whither, and it turned out that he also, like the journeyman tailor, was travelling without purpose, in the world. He said his name was Omar, that he was the nephew of Elfi Bey, the unfortunate bashaw of Cairo, and was now on his way to execute a commission which his uncle had delivered to him upon his dying-bed. Labakan was not so frank with respect to his circumstances; he gave him to understand that he was of lofty descent, and was travelling for pleasure.

The two young men were pleased with each other, and rode on in company. On the second day, Labakan interrogated his companion Omar, respecting the commission with which he was charged, and to his astonishment learned the following. Elfi Bey, the bashaw of Cairo, had brought up Omar from his earliest childhood; the young man had never known his parents. But shortly before, Elfi Bey, having been attacked by his enemies, and, after three disastrous engagements, mortally wounded, was obliged to flee, and disclosed to his charge that he was not his nephew, but the son of a powerful lord, who, inspired with fear by the prophecy of his astrologer, had sent the young prince away from his court, with an oath never to see him again until his twenty-second birthday. Elfi Bey had not told him his father's name, but had enjoined upon him with the greatest precision, on the fourth day of the coming month Ramadan, on which day he would be two-and-twenty years old, to repair to the celebrated pillar El-Serujah, four days' journey east of Alexandria: there he should offer to the men who would be standing by the pillar, a dagger which he gave him, with these words, "Here am I, whom ye seek!" If they answered, "Blessed be the Prophet, who has preserved thee!" then he was to follow them—they would lead him to his father.

The journeyman tailor, Labakan, was much astonished at this information; from this time he looked upon Prince Omar with envious eyes, irritated because fortune conferred upon him, though already he passed for the nephew of a mighty bashaw, the dignity of a king's son; but on him, whom she had endowed with all things necessary for a prince, bestowed in ridicule, an obscure lineage, and an every-day vocation. He instituted a comparison between himself and the prince. He was obliged to confess that the latter was a man of very lively aspect; that fine sparkling eyes belonged to him, a boldly-arched nose, a gentlemanly, complaisant demeanor, in a word, all the external accomplishments, which every one is wont to commend. But numerous as were the charms he found in his companion, still he was compelled to acknowledge to himself, that a Labakan would be no less acceptable to the royal father than the genuine prince.

These thoughts pursued Labakan the whole day; with them he went to sleep in the nearest night-lodgings; but when he awoke in the morning, and his eye rested upon Omar sleeping near him, who was reposing so quietly, and could dream of his now certain fortune, then arose in him the thought of gaining, by stratagem or violence, what unpropitious destiny had denied him. The dagger, the returning prince's token of recognition, hung in the sleeper's girdle; he softly drew it forth, to plunge it in the breast of its owner. Nevertheless, the peaceable soul of the journeyman recoiled before thoughts of murder; he contented himself with appropriating the dagger, and bridling for himself the faster horse of the prince; and, ere Omar awoke to see himself despoiled of all his hopes, his perfidious companion was several miles upon his way.

The day on which Labakan robbed the prince was the first of the holy month Ramadan, and he had therefore four days to reach the pillar El-Serujah, the locality of which was well known to him. Although the region wherein it was situated could at farthest be at a distance of but four days' journey, still he hastened to reach it, through a constant fear of being overtaken by the real prince.

By the end of the second day, he came in sight of the pillar El-Serujah. It stood upon a little elevation, in the midst of an extensive plain, and could be seen at a distance of two or three leagues. Labakan's heart beat high at the sight: though he had had time enough on horseback, for the last two days, to think of the part he was to play, still a consciousness of guilt made him anxious; the thought that he was born for a prince, however, encouraged him again, and he advanced towards the mark with renewed confidence.

The country around the pillar was uninhabited and desert, and the new prince would have experienced some difficulty in finding sustenance, if he had not previously supplied himself for several days. He lay down beside his horse beneath some palm-trees, and there awaited his distant destiny.

Towards the middle of the next day, he saw a large procession of horses and camels crossing the plain in the direction of the pillar El-Serujah. It reached the foot of the hill, on which the pillar stood; there they pitched splendid tents, and the whole looked like the travelling-suite of some rich bashaw or sheik. Labakan perceived that the numerous train which met his eye, had taken the pains to come hither on his account, and gladly would he that moment have shown them their future lord; but he mastered his eager desire to walk as prince; for, indeed, the next morning would consummate his boldest wishes.

The morning sun awoke the too happy tailor to the most important moment of his life, which would elevate him from an inferior situation, to the side of a royal father. As he was bridling his horse to ride to the pillar, the injustice of his course, indeed, occurred to him; his thoughts pictured to him the anguish of the true prince, betrayed in his fine hopes; but the die was cast: what was done could not be undone, and self-love whispered to him that he looked stately enough to pass for the son of the mightiest king. Inspirited by these reflections, he sprang upon his horse, and collecting all his courage to bring him to an ordinary gallop, in less than a quarter of an hour, reached the foot of the hill. He dismounted from his horse, and fastened it to one of the shrubs that were growing near; then he drew the dagger of Prince Omar, and proceeded up the hill. At the base of the pillar six persons were standing around an old gray-haired man, of lofty king-like aspect. A splendid caftan of gold cloth surrounded by a white Cashmere shawl, a snowy turban spangled with glittering precious stones, pointed him out as a man of opulence and nobility. To him Labakan proceeded, and bowing low before him, said, as he extended the dagger—

"Here am I, whom you seek."

"Praise to the Prophet who has preserved thee!" answered the gray-haired one, with tears of joy. "Omar, my beloved son, embrace thine old father!" The good tailor was deeply affected by these solemn words, and sank, with mingled emotions of joy and shame, into the arms of the old noble.

But only for a moment was he to enjoy the unclouded delight of his new rank; raising himself from the arms of the king, he saw a rider hastening over the plain in the direction of the hill. The traveller and his horse presented a strange appearance; the animal, either from obstinacy or fatigue, seemed unwilling to proceed. He went along with a stumbling gait, which was neither a pace nor a trot; but the rider urged him on, with hands and feet, to a faster run. Only too soon did Labakan recognise his horse Murva, and the real Prince Omar. But the evil spirit of falsehood once more prevailed within him, and he resolved, come what might, with unmoved front to support the rights he had usurped. Already, in the distance, had they observed the horseman making signs; at length, in spite of Murva's slow gait, having reached the bottom of the hill, he threw himself from his horse, and began rapidly to ascend.

"Hold!" cried he. "Hold! whoever you may be, and suffer not yourselves to be deceived by a most infamous impostor! I am called Omar, and let no mortal venture to misuse my name!"

Great astonishment was depicted on the countenances of the bystanders at this turn of the affair; the old man, in particular, seemed to be much amazed, as he looked inquiringly on one and another. Thereupon Labakan spoke, with a composure gained only by the most powerful effort.

"Most gracious lord and father, be not led astray by this man. He is, as far as I know, a mad journeyman tailor of Alexandria, by name Labakan, who deserves rather our pity than our anger."

These words excited the prince almost to phrensy. Foaming with passion, he would have sprung upon Labakan, but the bystanders, throwing themselves between, secured him, while the old man said: "Truly, my beloved son, the poor man is crazed. Let them bind him and place him on one of our dromedaries; perhaps we may be of some assistance to the unfortunate."

The anger of the prince had abated; in tears, he cried out to the old man, "My heart tells me that you are my father; by the memory of my mother, I conjure you—hear me!"

"Alas! God guard us!" answered he: "already he again begins to talk wildly. How can the man come by such crazy thoughts?" Thereupon, seizing Labakan's arm, he made him accompany him down the hill. They both mounted fine and richly-caparisoned coursers, and rode at the head of the procession, across the plain. They tied the hands of the unfortunate prince, however, and bound him securely upon a dromedary. Two horsemen rode constantly by his side, who kept a watchful eye upon his every movement.

The old prince was Saoud, sultan of the Wechabites. For some time had he lived without children; at last a prince, for whom he had so ardently longed, was born to him. But the astrologer, whom he consulted respecting the destiny of his son, told him that, until his twenty-second year, he would be in danger of being supplanted by an enemy. On that account, in order that he might be perfectly safe, had the sultan given him, to be brought up, to his old and tried friend, Elfi Bey; and twenty-two sad years had lived without looking upon him.

This did the sultan impart to his supposed son, and seemed delighted beyond measure with his figure and dignified demeanor.

When they reached the sultan's dominions, they were everywhere received by the inhabitants with shouts of joy; for the rumor of the prince's arrival had spread like wildfire through the cities and towns. In the streets through which they proceeded, arches of flowers and branches were erected; bright carpets of all colors adorned the houses; and the people loudly praised God and his prophet, who had discovered to them so noble a prince. All this filled the proud heart of the tailor with delight: so much the more unhappy did it make the real Omar, who, still bound, followed the procession in silent despair. In this universal jubilee, though it was all in his honor, no one paid him any attention. A thousand, and again a thousand, voices shouted the name of Omar; but of him who really bore this name, of him none took notice: at most, only one or two inquired whom they were carrying with them, so tightly bound, and frightfully in the ears of the prince sounded the answer of his guards, "It is a mad tailor."

The procession at last reached the capital of the sultan, where all was prepared for their reception with still more brilliancy than in the other cities. The sultana, an elderly woman of majestic appearance, awaited them, with her whole court, in the most splendid saloon of the castle. The floor of this room was covered with a large carpet; the walls were adorned with bright blue tapestry, which was suspended from massive silver hooks, by cords and tassels of gold.

It was dark by the time the procession came up, and accordingly many globular colored lamps were lighted in the saloon, which made night brilliant as day; but with the clearest brilliancy and most varied colors, shone those in the farthest part of the saloon, where the sultana was seated upon a throne. The throne stood upon four steps, and was of pure gold, inlaid with amethysts. The four most illustrious emirs held a canopy of crimson silk over the head of their mistress; and the sheik of Medina cooled her with a fan of peacock feathers. Thus awaited the sultana her husband and son; the latter she had never looked on since his birth, but significant dreams had so plainly shown her the object of her longings, that she would know him out of thousands.

Now they heard the noise of the approaching troop; trumpets and drums mingled with the huzzas of the populace; the hoofs of the horses sounded on the court of the palace; steps came nearer and nearer; the doors of the room flew open, and, through rows of prostrate attendants, hastened the sultan, holding his son by the hand, towards the mother's throne.

"Here," said he, "do I bring to thee, him for whom thou hast so often longed."

The sultana, however, interrupted him, crying: "This is not my son! These are not the features which the Prophet has shown me in my dreams!"

Just as the sultan was about to rebuke her superstition, the door of the saloon sprang open, and Prince Omar rushed in, followed by his guards, whom an exertion of his whole strength had enabled him to escape. Breathless, he threw himself before the throne, exclaiming:—

"Here will I die! Kill me, cruel father, for this disgrace I can endure no longer!"

All were confounded at these words; they pressed around the unfortunate one, and already were the guards, who had hurried up, on the point of seizing him and replacing his fetters, when the sultana, who had thus far looked on in mute astonishment, sprang from the throne.

"Hold!" she cried; "this, and no other, is my son! This is he, who, though my eyes have never seen him, is well known to my heart!" The guards had involuntarily fallen back from Omar, but the sultan, foaming with rage, commanded them to bind the madman.

"It is mine to decide," he cried with commanding tone; "and here we will judge, not by a woman's dreams, but by sure and infallible signs. This," pointing to Labakan, "is my son, for he has brought me the dagger, the real token of my friend Elfi."

"He stole it," cried Omar; "my unsuspicious confidence has he treacherously abused!" But the sultan hearkened not to the voice of his son, for he was wont in all things obstinately to follow his own judgment. He bade them forcibly drag the unfortunate Omar from the saloon, and himself retired with Labakan to his chamber, filled with anger at his wife, with whom, nevertheless, he had lived in happiness for five-and-twenty years. The sultana was full of grief at this affair; she was perfectly convinced that an impostor had taken possession of the sultan's heart, so numerous and distinct had been the dreams which pointed out the unhappy Omar as her son. When her sorrow had a little abated, she reflected on the means of convincing her husband of his mistake. This was indeed difficult, for he who had passed himself off as her son, had presented the dagger, the token of recognition, and had, moreover, as she learned, become acquainted with so much of Omar's early life from the lips of the prince himself, as to be able to play his part without betraying himself.

She called to her the men who had attended the sultan to the pillar El-Serujah, in order to have the whole matter exactly laid before her, and then took counsel with her most trusty female slaves. She chose, and in a moment rejected, this means and that; at length, Melechsalah, an old and cunning Circassian, spoke.

"If I have heard rightly, honored mistress, the one who bore this dagger called him whom thou holdest to be thy son, a crazy tailor, Labakan?"

"Yes, it is so," answered the sultana; "but what wilt thou make of that?"

"What think you," proceeded the slave, "of this impostor's having stitched his own name upon your son? If this be so, we have an excellent way of catching the deceiver, which I will impart to you in private."

The sultana gave ear to her slave, and the latter whispered to her a plan which seemed to please her, for she immediately got ready to go to the sultan. The sultana was a sensible woman, and knew not only the weak side of her husband, but also the way to take advantage of it. She seemed therefore to give up, and to be willing to acknowledge her son, only offering one condition: the sultan, whom the outbreak between himself and his wife had grieved, agreed thereto, and she said:—

"I would fain have from each a proof of his skill; another, perhaps, would have them contend in riding, in single conflict, or in hurling spears: but these are things which every one can do; I will give them something which will require both knowledge and dexterity. It shall be this; each shall make a caftan, and a pair of pantaloons, and then will we see at once who can make the finest ones."

The sultan laughingly answered, "Ah! thou hast hit on a fine expedient! Shall my son contend with a mad tailor, to see who can make the best caftan? No! that cannot be." The sultana, however, cried out, that he had already agreed to the condition, and her husband, who was a man of his word, at length yielded, though he swore, should the mad tailor make his caftan ever so beautiful, he would never acknowledge him as his son.

The sultan thereupon went to his son, and entreated him to submit to the caprices of his mother, who now positively wished to see a caftan from his hands. The heart of the good Labakan laughed with delight; if that be all that is wanting, thought he to himself, then shall the lady sultana soon behold me with joy. Two rooms had been fitted up, one for the prince, the other for the tailor; there were they to try their skill, and each was furnished with shears, needles, thread, and a sufficient quantity of silk.

The sultan was very eager to see what sort of a caftan his son would bring to light, but the heart of the sultana beat unquietly, from apprehension lest her stratagem might be unsuccessful. Two days had they been confined to their work; on the third, the sultan sent for his wife, and when she appeared, dispatched her to the apartments to bring the two caftans and their makers. With triumphant air Labakan walked in, and extended his garment before the astonished eyes of the sultan.

"Behold, father," said he, "look, mother! see if this be not a masterpiece of a caftan. I will leave it to the most skilful court-tailor, upon a wager, whether he can produce such another."

The sultana, smiling, turned to Omar:— "And thou, my son, what hast thou brought?"

Indignantly he cast the silk and shears upon the floor.

"They have taught me to tame horses, and to swing my sabre; and my lance will strike you a mark at sixty paces. But the art of the needle is unknown to me; it were unworthy a pupil of Elfi Bey, the lord of Cairo!"

"Oh, thou true son of my heart!" exclaimed the sultana. "Ah, that I might embrace thee, and call thee, son! Forgive me, husband and master," she continued, turning to the sultan, "for having set on foot this stratagem against you. See you not now who is prince, and who tailor? Of a truth the caftan which your lord son has made, is magnificent, and I would fain ask with what master he has learned!"

The sultan was lost in deep reflection, looking with distrust, now on his wife, now on Labakan, who vainly sought to conceal his blushes and consternation at having so stupidly betrayed himself. "This proof pleases me not," said he; "but, Allah be praised! I know a means of learning whether I am deceived." He commanded them to bring his swiftest horse, mounted, and rode to a forest, which commenced not far from the city. There, according to an old tradition, lived a good fairy, named Adolzaide, who had often before this assisted with her advice the monarchs of his family, in the hour of need: thither hastened the sultan.

In the middle of the wood was an open place, surrounded by lofty cedars. There, the story said, lived the fairy; and seldom did a mortal visit this spot, for a certain awe connected with it had, from olden time, descended from father to son. When the sultan had drawn near he dismounted, tied his horse to a tree, and placing himself in the middle of the open space, cried with loud voice:—

"If it be true that thou hast given good counsel to my fathers, in the hour of need, then disdain not the request of their descendant, and advise me in a case where human understanding is too short-sighted."

Hardly had he uttered the last word, when one of the cedars opened, and a veiled lady, in long white garments, stepped forth.

"I know, Sultan Saoud, why thou comest to me; thy wish is fair, therefore shall my assistance be thine. Take these two chests; let each of the two who claim to be thy son, choose; I know that he who is the real one, will not make a wrong selection." Thus speaking, the veiled lady extended to him two little caskets of ivory, richly adorned with gold and pearls: upon the lids, which he vainly sought to open, were inscriptions formed by inlaid diamonds.

As he was riding home, the sultan tormented himself with various conjectures, as to what might be the contents of the caskets, which, do his best, he could not open. The words on the outside threw no light upon the matter; for on one was inscribed, Honor and Fame; upon the other, Fortune and Wealth. Saoud thought it would be difficult to make choice between these two, which seemed equally attractive, equally alluring. When he reached the palace, he sent for his wife, and told her the answer of the fairy: it filled her with an eager hope, that he to whom her heart clung, might select the casket which would indicate his royal origin.

Two tables were brought in before the sultan's throne; on these, with his own hand, Saoud placed the two boxes; then, ascending to his seat, he gave the signal to one of his slaves to open the door of the saloon. A brilliant throng of bashaws and emirs of the realm poured through the open door: they seated themselves on the splendid cushions, which were arranged around the walls. When they had done this, Saoud gave a second signal, and Labakan was introduced; with haughty step he walked through the apartment, and prostrated himself before the throne with these words:—

"What is the command of my lord and father?" The sultan raised himself in his throne, and said:—

"My son, doubts are entertained as to the genuineness of thy claims to this name; one of these chests contains the confirmation of thy real birth. Choose! I doubt not thou wilt select the right one!" Labakan raised himself, and advanced towards the boxes; for a long time he reflected as to which he should choose, at last he said:—

"Honored father, what can be loftier than the fortune of being thy son? What more noble than the wealth of thy favor? I choose the chest which bears the inscription, Fortune And Wealth."

"We will soon learn whether thou hast made the right choice; meanwhile sit down upon that cushion, near the bashaw of Medina," said the sultan, again motioning to his slaves.

Omar was led in; his eye was mournful, his air dejected, and his appearance excited universal sympathy among the spectators. He threw himself before the throne, and inquired after the sultan's pleasure. Saoud informed him that he was to choose one of the chests: he arose, and approached the table. He read attentively both inscriptions, and said:—

"The few last days have informed me how insecure is fortune, how transient is wealth; but they have also taught me that, in the breast of the brave, lives what can never be destroyed, HONOR, and that the bright star of RENOWN sets not with fortune. The die is cast! should I resign a crown, Honor and Fame, you are my choice!" He placed his hand upon the casket that he had chosen, but the sultan commanded him not to unclose it, while he motioned to Labakan to advance, in like manner, before his table. He did so, and at the same time grasped his box. The sultan, however, had a chalice brought in, with water from Zemzem, the holy fountain of Mecca, washed his hands for supplication, and, turning his face to the East, prostrated himself in prayer:

"God of my fathers! Thou, who for centuries hast established our family, pure and unadulterated, grant that no unworthy one disgrace the name of the Abassidæ; be with thy protection near my real son, in this hour of trial." The sultan arose, and reascended his throne. Universal expectation enchained all present; they scarcely breathed; one could have heard a mouse crawl over the hall, so mute and attentive were all. The hindmost extended their necks, in order to get a view of the chests, over the heads of those in front. The sultan spoke: "Open the chests;" and they, which before no violence could force, now sprang open of their own accord.

In the one which Omar had chosen, lay upon a velvet cushion, a small golden crown, and a sceptre: in Labakan's, a large needle, and a little linen thread. The sultan commanded both to bring their caskets before him: he took the little crown from the cushion in his hand, and, wonderful to see! it became larger and larger, until it reached the size of a real crown. Placing it on his son Omar, who kneeled before him, he kissed his forehead, and bade him sit upon his right hand. To Labakan, however, he turned and said:—

"There is an old proverb, 'Shoemaker, stick to thy last;' it seems that thou shouldst stick to thy needle. Thou hast not, indeed, merited much mercy at my hands, but one has supplicated for thee, whom this day I can refuse nothing; therefore give I thee thy paltry life; but, if I may advise, haste thee to leave my land."

Ashamed, ruined as he was, the poor tailor could answer nothing: he threw himself before the prince, and tears came into his eyes.

"Can you forgive me, prince?" he said.

"To be true to a friend, magnanimous to a foe, is the pride of the Abassidæ!" answered the prince, raising him. "Go in peace!"

"My true son!" cried the old sultan, deeply affected, and sinking upon Omar's breast. The emirs and bashaws, and all the nobles of the realm, arose from their seats, to welcome the new prince, and amid this universal jubilee, Labakan, his chest under his arm, crept out of the saloon.

He went down into the sultan's stable, bridled his horse Murva, and rode forth from the gate towards Alexandria. His whole career as prince recurred to him as a dream, and the splendid chest, richly adorned with pearls and diamonds, alone convinced him that it was not all an idle vision. Having at last reached Alexandria, he rode to the house of his old master, dismounted, and fastening his horse to the door, walked into the workshop. The master, who did not even know him, made a low bow and asked what was his pleasure: when, however, he had a nearer view of his guest, and recognised his old Labakan, he called to his journeymen and apprentices, and all precipitated themselves, like mad, upon poor Labakan, who expected no such reception; they bruised and beat him with smoothing-irons and yard-sticks, pricked him with needles, and pinched him with sharp shears, until he sank down, exhausted, on a heap of old clothes. As he lay there, the master ceased, for a moment, from his blows, to ask after the stolen garments: in vain Labakan assured him that he had come back on that account alone, to set all right; in vain offered him threefold compensation for his loss; the master and his journeymen fell upon him again, beat him terribly, and turned him out of doors. Sore and bruised, he mounted Murva, and rode to a caravansery. There he laid down his weary lacerated head, reflecting on the sorrows of earth, on merit so often unrewarded, and on the nothingness and transientness of all human blessings. He went to sleep with the determination to give up all hopes of greatness, and to become an honest burgher. Nor on the following day did he repent of his resolution, for the heavy hands of his master, and the journeymen, had cudgelled out of him all thoughts of nobility.

He sold his box to a jeweller for a high price, and fitted up a workshop for his business. When he had arranged all, and had hung out, before his window, a sign with the inscription, Labakan, Merchant Tailor, he sat down and began with the needle and thread he had found in the chest, to mend the coat which his master had so shockingly torn. He was called off from his work, but on returning to it, what a wonderful sight met his eyes! The needle was sewing industriously away, without being touched by any one; it took fine, elegant stitches, such as Labakan himself had never made even in his most skilful moments.

Truly the smallest present of a kind fairy is useful, and of great value! Still another good quality had the gift; be the needle as industrious as it might, the little stock of thread never gave out.

Labakan obtained many customers, and was soon the most famous tailor for miles around. He cut out the garments, and took the first stitch therein with the needle, and immediately the latter worked away, without cessation, until the whole was completed. Master Labakan soon had the whole city for customers, for his work was beautiful, and his charges low; and only one thing troubled the brains of the people of Alexandria, namely, how he finished his work entirely without journeymen, and with closed doors.

Thus was the motto of the chest which promised fortune and

wealth undergoing its accomplishment. Fortune and Wealth accompanied, with gradual increase, the steps of the good tailor, and when he listened to the praises of the young sultan Omar, who lived in every mouth; when he heard that this brave man was the object of his people's pride and love, the terror of his enemies; then would the quondam prince say to himself, "Still is it better that I remained a tailor, for Honor and Fame are ever accompanied by danger."

Thus lived Labakan, contented with himself, respected by his fellow-burghers; and if the needle, meanwhile, has not lost her cunning, she is still sewing with the everlasting thread of the good Fairy Adolzaide.

At sundown the Caravan set out, and soon reached Birket-el-had, or "the Pilgrims' Fountain," whence the distance to Cairo was three leagues. The Caravan had been expected at this time, and the merchants soon had the pleasure of seeing their friends coming forth from the city to meet them. They entered through the gate Bebel-Falch, for it was considered a good omen for those who came from Mecca to enter by this gate, because the Prophet himself had passed through it.

At the market-place the four Turkish merchants took leave of the stranger and the Greek Zaleukos, and went home with their friends. Zaleukos, however, showed his companion a good caravansery, and invited him to dine with him. The stranger agreed, and promised to make his appearance as soon as he should have changed his dress. The Greek made every arrangement for giving a fine entertainment to the stranger, for whom, upon the journey, he had conceived a deep feeling of esteem; and when the meats and drink had been brought in in proper order, he seated himself, waiting for his guest.

He heard slow and heavy steps approaching through the gallery which led to their apartment. He arose in order to meet him as a friend, and welcome him upon the threshold; but, full of horror, he started back as the door opened—the same frightful Red-mantle walked in before him! His eyes were still turned upon him; it was no illusion: the same lofty, commanding figure, the mask, from beneath which shone forth the dark eyes, the red cloak with embroidery of gold—all were but too well known to him, impressed upon his mind as they had been during the most awful moments of his life.

The breast of Zaleukos heaved with contending emotions; he had long since felt reconciled towards this too-well-remembered apparition, and forgiven him; nevertheless his sudden appearance opened every wound afresh. All those torturing hours of anguish, that wo which had envenomed the bloom of his life, rushed back for a moment, crowding upon his soul.

"What wishest thou, terrible one?" cried the Greek, as the apparition still stood motionless upon the threshold. "Away with thee, that I may curse thee not!"

"Zaleukos!" said a well-known voice from under the mask: "Zaleukos! is it thus that you receive your guest?" The speaker removed the mask, and threw back his cloak: it was Selim Baruch, the stranger! But still Zaleukos seemed not at ease, for he too plainly recognised in him the Unknown of the Ponte Vecchio: nevertheless, old habits of hospitality conquered; he silently motioned to the stranger to seat himself at the table.

"I can guess your thoughts," commenced the latter, when they had taken their places: "your eyes look inquiringly upon me. I might have been silent, and your gaze would never more have beheld me; but I owe you an explanation, and therefore did I venture to appear before you in my former guise, even at the risk of receiving your curse. You once said to me, 'The faith of my fathers bids me love him; and he is probably more unhappy than myself:' be assured of this, my friend, and listen to my justification.

"I must begin far back, in order that you may fully understand my story. I was born in Alexandria, of Christian parents. My father, the youngest son of an ancient illustrious French family, was consul for his native land in the city I have just mentioned. From my tenth year I was brought up in France, by one of my mother's brothers, and left my fatherland for the first time a few years after the revolution broke out there, in company with my uncle, who was no longer safe in the land of his ancestors, in order to seek refuge with my parents beyond the sea. We landed eagerly, hoping to find in my father's house the rest and quiet of which the troubles of France had deprived us. But ah! in my father's house I found not all as it should be: the external storms of these stirring times had not, it is true, reached it; but the more unexpectedly had misfortune made her home in the inmost hearts of my family. My brother, a promising young man, first secretary of my father, had shortly before married a young lady, the daughter of a Florentine noble who lived in our vicinity: two days before our arrival she had suddenly disappeared, and neither our family nor her own father could discern the slightest trace of her. At last they came to the conclusion that she had ventured too far in a walk, and had fallen into the hands of robbers. Almost agreeable was this thought to my poor brother, when compared to the truth, which only too soon became known. The perfidious one had eloped with a young Neapolitan, with whom she had become acquainted in her father's house. My brother, who was exceedingly affected by this step, employed every means to bring the guilty one to punishment; but in vain: his attempts, which in Naples and Florence had excited wonder, served only to complete his and our misfortune. The Florentine nobleman returned to his native land, under the pretence of seeing justice done to my brother, but with the real determination of destroying us all. He frustrated all those examinations which my brother had set on foot, and knew how to use his influence, which he had obtained in various ways, so well, that my father and brother fell under suspicion of their government, were seized in the most shameful manner, carried to France, and there suffered death by the axe of the executioner. My poor mother lost her mind; and not until ten long months had passed, did death release her from her awful situation, though for the few last days she was possessed of perfect consciousness. Thus did I now stand isolated in the world: one thought alone occupied my whole soul, one thought alone bade me forget my sorrows; it was the mighty flame which my mother in her last moments had kindled within me.

"In her last moments, as I said, recollection returned; she had me summoned, and spoke with composure of our fate, and her own death. Then she sent all out of the room, raised herself, with a solemn air, from her miserable bed, and said that I should receive her blessing, if I would swear to accomplish something with which she would charge me. Amazed at the words of my dying mother, I promised with an oath to do whatever she should tell me. She thereupon broke forth in imprecations against the Florentine and his daughter, and charged me, with the most frightful threats of her curse, to avenge upon him the misfortunes of my house. She died in my arms. This thought of vengeance had long slumbered in my soul; it now awoke in all its might. I collected what remained of my paternal property, and bound myself by an oath to stake it all upon revenge, and, rather than be unsuccessful, to perish in the attempt.

"I soon arrived in Florence, where I kept myself as private as possible; it was very difficult to put my plan in execution on account of the situation which my enemy occupied. The old Florentine had become governor, and thus had in his hand all the means of destroying me, should he entertain the slightest suspicion. An accident came to my assistance. One evening I saw a man in well-known livery, walking through the streets: his uncertain gait, his gloomy appearance, and the muttered 'Santo sacramento,' and 'Maledetto diavolo,' soon made me recognise old Pietro, a servant of the Florentine, whom I had formerly known in Alexandria. There was no doubt but that he was in a passion with his master, and I resolved to turn his humor to my advantage. He appeared much surprised to see me there, told me his grievances, that he could do nothing aright for his master since he had become governor, and my gold supported by his anger soon brought him over to my side. Most of the difficulty was now removed: I had a man in my pay, who would open to me at any hour the doors of my enemy, and from this time my plan of vengeance advanced to maturity with still greater rapidity. The life of the old Florentine seemed to me too pitiful a thing, to be put into the balance with that of my whole family. Murdered before him, he must see the dearest object of his love, and this was his daughter Bianca. It was she that had so shamefully wronged my brother, it was she that had been the author of our misfortunes. My heart, thirsting for revenge, eagerly drank in the intelligence, that Bianca was on the point of being married a second time; it was settled—she must die. But as my soul recoiled at the deed, and I attributed too little nerve to Pietro, we looked around for a man to accomplish our fell design. I could hire no Florentine, for there was none that would have undertaken such a thing against the governor. Thereupon Pietro hit upon a plan, which I afterwards adopted, and he thereupon proposed you, being a foreigner and a physician, as the proper person. The result you know: only, through your excessive foresight and honesty, my undertaking seemed, at one time, to be tottering; hence the scene with the mantle.

"Pietro opened for us the little gate in the governor's palace; he would have let us out, also, in the same secret manner, if we had not fled, overcome by horror at the frightful spectacle, which, through the crack of the door, presented itself to our eyes. Pursued by terror and remorse, I ran on about two hundred paces, until I sank down upon the steps of a church. There I collected myself again, and my first thought was of you, and your awful fate, if found within the house.

"I crept back to the palace, but neither of Pietro nor yourself could I discover a single trace. The door, however, was open, and I could at least hope that you had not neglected this opportunity of flight.

"But when the day broke, fear of detection, and an

unconquerable feeling of remorse, allowed me to remain no longer within the walls of Florence. I hastened to Rome. Imagine my consternation, when, after a few days, the story was everywhere told, with the addition that, in a Grecian physician, they had detected the murderer. In anxious fear, I returned to Florence; my vengeance now seemed too great: I cursed it again and again, for with your life it was purchased all too dearly. I arrived on the same day which cost you a hand. I will not tell you what I felt, when I saw you ascend the scaffold, and bear all with such heroism. But when the blood gushed forth in streams, then was my resolution taken, to sweeten the rest of your days. What has since happened you know; it only now remains to tell you, why I have travelled with you. As the thought that you had never yet forgiven me, pressed heavily upon me, I determined to spend some days with you, and at last to give you an explanation of what I had done."

Silently had the Greek listened to his guest; with a kind look, as he finished, he offered him his right hand.

"I knew very well that you must be more unhappy than I, for that awful deed will, like a thick cloud, forever darken your days. From my heart I forgive you. But answer me yet one question: how came you under this form, in the wilderness? What did you set about, after purchasing my house in Constantinople?"

"I returned to Alexandria," answered the guest. "Hate against all mankind raged in my bosom; burning hate, in particular, against that people, whom they call 'the polished nation.' Believe me, my Moslem friends pleased me better. Scarcely a month had I been in Alexandria, when the invasion of my countrymen took place. I saw in them only the executioners of my father and brother; I, therefore, collected some young people of my acquaintance, who were of the same mind as myself, and joined those brave Mamelukes, who were so often the terror of the French host. When the campaign was finished, I could not make up my mind to return to the peaceful arts. With my little band of congenial friends, I led a restless, careless life, devoted to the field and the chase. I live contented among this people, who honor me as their chief; for though my Asiatics are not quite so refined as your Europeans, yet are they far removed from envy and slander, from selfishness and ambition."

Zaleukos thanked the stranger for his relation, but did not conceal from him, that he would find things better suited to his rank and education, if he would live and work in Christian, in European lands. With delight his companion looked upon him.

"I know by this," said he, "that you have entirely forgiven me, that you love me: receive, in return, my heartfelt thanks." He sprang up, and stood in full height before the Greek, whom the warlike air, the dark sparkling eyes, the deep mysterious voice of his guest, almost inspired with fear. "Thy proposal is intended kindly," continued he; "for another it might have charms; but I—I cannot accept it. Already stands my horse saddled: already do my attendants await me. Farewell, Zaleukos!"

The friends whom destiny had so strangely thrown together, embraced at parting. "And how may I call thee? What is the name of my guest, who will forever live in my remembrance?" exclaimed the Greek.

The stranger gazed at him some time, and said, as he pressed his hand once more: "They call me 'the lord of the wilderness;' I am the Robber Orbasan!"

THE END

S.

Made in the USA
Las Vegas, NV
28 October 2021

33213659R00069